Verge 2023

Verge 2023

Defiant

Edited by
Samuel Bernard, Thomas Rock and Vera Yingzhi Gu

MONASH
UNIVERSITY
PUBLISHING

Published by Monash University Publishing
Matheson Library Annexe
40 Exhibition Walk
Monash University
Clayton, Victoria 3800, Australia
publishing.monash.edu/

Monash University Publishing: the discussion starts here

Verge 2023: Defiant

ISSN: 2208-5637

ISBN: 9781922633750 (paperback)
ISBN: 9781922633767 (pdf)
ISBN: 9781922633774 (epub)

A catalogue record for this
book is available from the
National Library of Australia

Typesetting by Jo Mullins
Design by Les Thomas
Cover design by Les Thomas
Cover image by Midjourney
'Chimaera' illustration © 2023 Elena Disilvestro

Printed in Australia by Griffin Press

Contents

CONTENTS

Introduction

Defiance is too often associated with rebellion, insurrection or revolution, though the act is exquisitely heterogeneous. For Verge's 2023 issue, we challenged writers to ponder this timely and universal concept. In doing so, we continue the proud tradition, which now stretches seventeen years, of publishing remarkable stories and poems from emerging and established writers.

It's a difficult task to balance theme and creative endeavour; too much of either and the work flounders, estranged from either goal. Each word must be precise, every space evaluated, and the voice must hold the reader's attention. The following thirty-one pieces for *Verge 2023* were selected not only because of their relevance to the theme but also because each piece is distinct in its own artistic pursuit. Every author has taken the theme and run with it in their own way, creating a collection of voices unified by one idea.

Almost a year ago, the editorial team met to discuss potential themes, eager to carry on the tradition of past editions. 'Defiant' and 'defiance' resonated with us early on, and we chose the former hoping it would inspire more domestic, personal fiction rather than epic stories with climaxes of grand acts of defiance. Our hopes were met. Inside *Verge 2023* are stories and poems about futures and pasts, set in homes, forests and drowned cities. Stories of kindness and cruelty, poems of brutality and hope; but above all, of a defiant act, a testament to the enduring human spirit. And very often, the stories are of defiant women seeking a better life in futures and other worlds, behind the screen, on our streets and in our homes.

It is no easy task to share that very personal part of yourself – your imagination. To the *Verge 2023* writers, we thank you for inviting us into your worlds.

We are exceptionally proud of this literary journal, and we hope that the defiant acts that follow will resonate and inspire.

Verge 2023 *editorial team*

1

Bouzouki

Warwick Sprawson

I was in the garden pulling weeds when my elderly neighbour George shuffled down the driveway. In his 80s, he was lean and craggy, with wiry grey hair and fingers thick from a lifetime's hard work.

'Olrigh?' he asked, his standard greeting, and one of his few words of English.

'Good,' I replied, my standard reply.

Then, as usual, he launched into a lengthy discourse in Greek. That's the way it went with George and me; he spoke in Greek and I didn't understand a word; I replied in English and he didn't understand a word. Somehow it worked, and we often ended up having long in-depth conversations.

George looked around my garden, seeming to search for something, then pointed at the Western Australian peppermint tree and made slicing motions, talking in Greek the whole time.

My understanding of what George was talking about was based on his tone, hand gestures and facial expressions. If he sounded relatively upbeat I usually assumed he was talking about his vegetable garden. While most of George's extensive backyard was full of small homemade sheds – six or seven tenuous structures made of rusted corrugated iron, roofs weighed down by stones and old tyres – there were vegetable beds between the sheds, the rich soil yielding lush beans, tomatoes, eggplants, zucchinis and basil. I worked from home, and from my window desk I watched George patiently tend his plants: spreading compost, forking the soil, watering, tying up seedlings and picking fruit, all the while listening to an ancient radio playing old Greek songs.

When George sounded angry and flung his hands towards his house I guessed he was complaining about his wife, Sotiria. Sotiria wore thick oval-framed glasses and moved with the rocking motion of someone with bad hips. Apart from going to church and the local shops, she seemed to rarely leave home. The few times I had encountered her she had smiled and waved, radiating quiet kindness, and I wondered how she came to marry such as irascible individual as George. Like a scheduled event, just about every evening George and Sotiria had an epic argument, her voice high, wavery and indignant, his voice low and loaded with fury. They shouted back and forth for five or ten minutes like some kind of verbal tennis match, then, game over for the night, fell silent.

George walked over to the peppermint tree and turned his hand into an imaginary chainsaw, making chainsaw sounds as he cut vertical slices from the trunk. This was another of his favourite subjects. George hated the tree. He had been at me for years to cut it down, perhaps because it shaded his backyard in the afternoon. When George raised the issue of the tree I liked to pretend I didn't understand what he was talking about.

'Yes, nice tree isn't it. A good one!'

George scowled and made vigorous sawing motions into his palm.

'You're quite right, the rainbow lorikeets love it. It's great habitat.'

Making an exasperated '*ba*' sound, George looked about the garden then gestured for me to follow him with a single curl of his palm-down fingers. He led me into my own garage, where he peered around, poking through the bits of wood leaning against the wall.

'What is it? What are you after?'

He found a coffee-table sized piece of plywood. He looked it over and nodded.

'You want some plywood? You can have that bit. That's leftover from the shelves.' I pushed the plywood towards him.

'No,' he said firmly. After ruminating for a while he said, 'More'.

He curled a cupped hand at me and I followed him to my station wagon parked in the driveway. He touched the roof racks. 'More'.

'You want me to drive you somewhere to buy plywood?' I asked.

He nodded and – a rarity – smiled. When George smiled he was transformed from an irritable old man into a slightly less irritable old man. 'Good,' he said, clapping me on the shoulder and opening the car's passenger door.

It wasn't the first time George had asked me to drive him somewhere. A few months before he had – after a lengthy game of charades – got me to drive him to Aldi. I wasn't sure why he wanted to go to the supermarket, but it turned out potting mix was on special. He directed me to load eight 20 kilo bags onto the trolley. At the checkout he walked past the line of waiting people to the front of the queue, waving exasperatedly for me to join him.

When the neighbours across the road were renovating, George would wait until the builders had left for the day. Then he would come over to my house, rap powerfully on the door and get me to help lug heavy lumps of concrete out of his backyard and into the builders' skip.

I found his intrusions both annoying and entertaining. I was a freelance bid writer. George knew I worked from home. Besides my work I didn't have much going on in my life, and I liked it that way. Although I didn't like being interrupted, I was more than repaid for helping George with the occasional errand. About once a week he would come to the door and hand over a bag of whatever was in season. Lately it had been nectarines, figs and tomatoes. Disdainfully waving away my thanks he would shuffle back up the drive.

Most of what I knew about George I learned from Daphne at the end of the street. She was in her 90s, and had lived in Garden Street since 1963. Her husband had died and her sons rarely visited, so Daphne spent her days sitting in a seat next to her mailbox, chatting to people walking past. Over the years she'd gleaned bits and pieces on George and Sotiria, both from her own observations and from a Greek-speaking friend who attended the same Greek Orthodox Church. George had been a fisherman in Greece before emigrating to Australia in the late 1950s. In 1961 he met Sotiria in Melbourne, another recent Greek émigré, getting married before moving into Garden Street in 1965. George rode his bike to work at the same industrial cleaning supply warehouse until he retired around 20 years ago. George and his wife had never had a driver's licence, never learnt more than a few words of English and never had children. Apparently George had never wanted to live in this industrial inland suburb, he wanted to live by the sea.

I drove George to the McKays Hardware where I had bought my plywood. George directed me to add a 2 meter length of plywood sheet onto the roof racks, and then another one and another one, until we had six sheets. 'Do you really need all this? What are you making? Another shed?'

George paid for the plywood, and I drove around to the alley behind his house. He wrangled open an old roller door and I leant the plywood against the back fence.

The next day there was a screeching sound and a huge clattering crash. From my desk I could see one of George's sheds had collapsed. I rushed outside and looked over the fence. He was busy with a crowbar, wrenching roofing nails from corrugated iron. 'Olrigh!' he said cheerily, stacking the rusty iron sheets in one pile and the shed's wooden beams into another.

Over the next week George demolished all the other sheds in his backyard, making four massive piles in the centre of his yard: the plywood we had bought, corrugated iron sheets, wooden beams and miscellaneous junk, from broken buckets to empty olive oil tins.

That Saturday George came around early. He looked over the fence at his own place and pointed to the pile of junk. Then he pointed to my car.

'The tip?' I asked wearily.

He put a hand on my shoulder and squeezed gently.

We parked in the alley and dragged the rubbish – old car tyres, cracked plant pots, broken appliances, three legged seats, rusted bikes – out through the roller door. George did his share of work; he might be doddery on his legs, but he was still surprisingly strong.

It took three carloads, including filling the roof racks, to clear it out. Fortunately George kept the corrugated iron and most of the wood from the demolished sheds.

On the way back from our third tip run George got me to stop at Fabric Warehouse. We went inside and he bought an entire bolt of white polyester fabric. Driving home I asked him why he wanted so much cloth. As far as I could work out, George was going to rebuild a shed, larger and better than the old ones, from the old shed materials. He would use the cloth to line the interior, a cheap alternative to plaster.

The next day George set four wooden poles vertically in the ground. He tacked the polyester sheet to the poles, screening off a 10 metres square space from view in the centre of his yard. The space enclosed the piles of plywood, wooden beams and corrugated iron.

I didn't see George much for the next month, although I heard him plenty, sawing, drilling and hammering from behind his white screen. Now and then a bit of wood poked above the white fabric. Sometimes he'd make a trip to the house for tools or a snack. His radio was on all day, scratchy Greek tunes full of the intricate chatter of the bouzouki.

In the evening, like usual, the arguments between George and Sotiria would start up, the two of them yelling at each other with a passion of a far younger couple.

One Saturday morning George walked up the drive carrying a splattered can of white paint. He raised the can before him, lifting it with one finger, indicating that it was empty. Then he pointed to the car.

I knew the drill. I sighed and fetched my car keys.

At McKays, George bought three 10 litre cans of white paint, three 10 litre cans of blue paint, two paint brushes and another six pieces of plywood.

I noticed he was moving slower and letting me do more of the lifting. 'Are you okay? What are you doing anyway? Why on earth do you need all this stuff?'

'Olrigh,' he said gruffly, checking the knots tying the plywood to the roof racks.

After another week or so the hammering and sawing mostly stopped, replaced by the faint headachy smell of wet paint.

George emerged from the screen with a piece of corrugated iron. He carried the iron sheet to the far side of the yard near the alley and placed it flat on the ground. The face up side was painted blue. Over the next few days George methodically covered every square inch of the backyard with the blue painted corrugated iron. The metal rose slightly where it covered his vegetable beds. When George walked over the metal it made a huge crumping noise, scaring birds into flight.

By this stage I was spending more and more time sitting at my desk looking over the fence and wondering what George was doing, and less and less time actually working.

A couple of days later I had just sat back at my desk with a cup of tea when George appeared outside the fabric screen with a tall metal prop. He stepped onto a milk crate and hammered the prop into the ground before disappearing behind the screen again. A short time later, the end of a thick pole emerged above the screen, coming to rest on the prop at a 20 degree angle. After a few minutes the pole began to rise in steady increments, hoisted by a rope attached at the top of the pole. The pole – some 5 metres high – came to rest vertically in the centre of George's enclosure.

I waited for a flag to be raised, but for awhile nothing else happened. I'd just come back from the kitchen with some toast when one of the poles holding the fabric screen wobbled and was pulled from the ground. I saw George wrestle with it, material still attached, until he managed to suspended the pole horizontally. It was hard to see exactly what was going on, as the remaining fabric partly screened him from view. Part of the fabric attached to the horizontal pole began to inch upwards, pulled by a rope at the top of the flagpole, rising into the air like a giant curtain. As the white material reached the top of the flagpole, the remaining fabric broke away from the remaining three stakes, revealing what was behind.

In the centre of George's yard was a 10 metre long, dazzling white boat. The plywood boat's raised prow swooped down to a wide hull, splayed open like a pair of cupped hands. The mast was set about three metres from the bow, in front of a small plywood wheelhouse in the centre of the deck. Beneath the bow was painted a blue eye, the top of the iris hidden beneath a fierce black eyelid.

George finished hauling up the sail and tied the rope fast. The sail snapped and rippled in the breeze. He walked slowly across the boat's deck to the wheelhouse where he gripped the wheel, standing as still and stern as a figurehead, at peace, looking over the rippling blue sea.

2

Exiting the Forest

Cameron Semmens

When returning (as you must)
to the world of subtle fists, missed calls,
and the crawling fear of environmental apocalypse
try to remember
the tenacity of tree ferns
(their fingering fronds
and tender, tickling fiddleheads
have lasted millions of years).
Try to let your thoughts settle like leaf litter
(only in such stillness
does lushness emerge),
and try to let your rock-hard convictions
remember the transformative weight
of a trickling stream.

When re-dressing yourself (as you must)
in life's polyester responsibilities
perhaps, leave the top button of your shirt
undone (a hint of the naked animal you are).
Perhaps, souvenir a fresh gum leaf to be crumpled up
when that next odorous thing really gets up your nose.
Perhaps, imagine the small seed of a mountain ash
implanting itself in the rich soil of your dark thoughts,

imagine watering it with your tears,
imagine it sprouting and flourishing,
with every *twig* expanding
into whole new branches of possibility.

When leaving (as you must)
the shade of many trees,
remember this:
the thick forest canopy is a shield
to a teeming army of light-shy life.
And maybe,
in the darkness you know beyond
(and the gloom you carry within),
there is a wild life
that *needs* the dabbled darkness to thrive.

3

Spider in the Woods

Isabelle Quilty

This morning there is soil beneath my fingernails, and the taste of blood lingers on my lips. My husband kisses me, sleepily, and either doesn't notice or doesn't care. I'm not sure what scares me more. For the past month, in what my poor memory allows me, my morning has been much the same. I writhe, naked, beneath his grip until the sun has cloaked both of our naked bodies entirely and his head falls into my shoulder with a shudder. I then wander down to the kitchen at a sloth's pace, a finger tracing the places where his teeth met my neck. The machine whirs, the smell of coffee fills the kitchen and I drink the water from the farm's old pipes.

This place carries my husband's grandfather's bones. He was a war hero of some kind, pinned with medals and left to wither in this farmhouse for all the years since his wife's passing. I'm convinced the man murdered his wife, but I never let my suspicions slip. Some things are better left unsaid.

The coffee machine chimes with a cheery tune. The morning dew races down the kitchen window panes and just beyond the opaque glass, I see the garden. There was once a rose bush that sat beneath the window, and seeing the red and whites was the highlight of my day. The thorns, roots, and flowers have all been torn up. In its place, a freshly filled in hole of upturned soil. The very same soil beneath my fingernails.

The blood.

The blood.

Is this where life begins?

Underneath the bed of soil, beneath the thorns and roots of the roses, does life push forth, harsh and thorough?

I hold onto the countertop. Whose house is this? The striped linen dress is a mockery. A falsehood of what could've been.

This dream doesn't taste right. It punctures a tender part of me. The picturesque. The longing for the pastoral, of green fields, water with history, and a husband to warm my bed. But I never belonged here. I am not the daughter of a farmer, with doe eyes and a kind heart.

I live beneath stone, soil, and thorns. I am a prisoner within my kingdom, a daughter of the defeated god. They keep me here with a collar around my neck, with stone designed to keep such horror contained. Here I sleep. Here I dream of all manner of creatures in the woods.

I see an heiress. Her skin is a milky white with hair black as night and thin eyes. Red and gold paint her body, and all the wealth in the world plays at her fingertips. She has all she could ever wish for, and those around her salivate. Their teeth scrape over the flesh and this dream is soured. She is another piece of the property, prettily draped over the sun lounge. Men will trade her all her life, and she will be expected to thank them. Her wealth was never truly hers. Another plaything. A hand pushes her head down and asks her to choke.

The dream lies in shreds, like the remains of a dress. I don't return to the prison beneath the Earth. Instead, I am thrown back into the farmhouse. To the woman with milky white skin, hair dark as night, and thin eyes. The afternoon has bled onto the horizon. The coffee machine chimes. His afternoon coffee is ready. I pour a cup for him, in a crudely made clay mug his little brother made for him. I go to pour one for myself, but he stops me with a gentle hand against my stomach.

No. Think of our boy.

Whose child is this?

I remember the cream and sugar, and I turn away. A droplet of coffee rolls down my finger from the lip of the cup. I lap it up with a long, curious swipe of my tongue. A rush of fire rolls through my body, right beneath my skin. I can't let him see.

I sit beside him obediently as he sips his coffee. 'How are the tests going?' He asks. There is a ghost of an itch where a collar might sit around my neck.

'The tests?' I echo. There's a distant air about me whenever words leave my lips.

He cocks his head. The coffee pours from the cup.

'You've always been resistant to sedatives, haven't you?' He sounds like he's speaking to me from the end of a long, empty hall. I want to cup the side of his face and run my fingers through the rough feeling of his beard. But I cannot touch him. Not when he's asking me questions like this.

I settle on whispering. 'Did you see the rose garden yet?'

He clears his throat. His impatience is suffocating.

'I *said*, you've always been resistant to sedatives, haven't you? We'll have to up the dosage. A needle doesn't go through rock so easily, after all,' He says. He taps the top of his clipboard with the tip of his pen. It's metal, ballpoint. I got it for his birthday, I think.

I escape to the kitchen and brace myself against the counter. The sink is filled, not with water, but with rose petals. I crave the feeling and dip my fingers into the depths. They surface, and now my fingers, once white and pure, are sheathed in blood.

This dream is breaking, but I'm desperate. It's always been my favourite.

'What have you done, now?' My husband's voice is gentle, but the crocodile threat in his voice lingers just below the surface. He turns me around, and now I'm pressed between him and the counter.

He's holding my shoulders now.

The dream isn't meant to be like this.

This place is honey and roses. This place is morning sex and absinthe. But now he's speaking back to me, reaching through the film coating the waters of lucidity and lust. To awaken would mean to acknowledge my prison. I cannot abide that. He lashes out and tears at my dress. There is not flesh and lace beneath, but another dream.

I see her, a waitress. She wears a blue uniform, her hands dirty and sore, and the diner is empty. Lights flicker in the street outside. No one lingers in the parking lot, but she feels a presence. A knock on the glass door. There. He was waiting for the last family to leave. When I first crafted this dream, it was all cream, filtered coffee, and doughnuts. Soon, I began to feel his presence. The spider with a smile. Sharp teeth and sultry words fill his mouth. He claims I owe him. I have a debt to pay.

There is always a debt to pay. These dreams have soured, become crooked, and faded. Cloaked in a shadow I don't know how to untangle or discern.

He knocks again, claws rapping on the glass.

There is always a debt.

My fingertips are sore from cleaning the hot cups, and washing the dishes. I glance down and see that my fingertips are coated in blood. One after the other, these dreams are shattering, returning to sand between my fingers. I'm beginning to feel the stone around me begin to press in. The desperation is getting worse, and I throw myself back into the dream of my husband and the farm house. Opening my eyes I find myself sitting in the old armchair, twilight fluttering through the blinds. The stripes of light cross over my body like bars in the jail cell.

I don't remember this part of the dream. A faint tapping sounds from the empty fireplace. It grows louder until I cannot bear it any longer, and I investigate the chimney. With the faint light, it's near impossible to see anything properly.

Click, click, click.

I see it. A caterpillar-like creature with the face of a smiling, long-fanged cat is worming its way down to me. The sound of the clicking is its great black mandibles scratching the blackened brick. It opens its horrible mouth.

'I have given you everything. I fought for you, for your freedom. *Pitiful creature, pitiful creature...*' The creature's voice is that of an old man with a heavy rasp. War medals dangle from its twitching body. It closes its mouth and pauses, as though in thought. Then, it launches itself at me. I scramble away and I drop below the floorboards as though the wood is nothing more than air and I find myself packed between the floorboards and the dirt.

A woman, long-dead, lays beside me. She's little more than a skeleton, her once-beautiful dress in tatters. She turns and looks to me, sympathy in her eye-sockets. She holds my hand, offering the little comfort she can. It means the world. Her bone fingertips brush mine and I can tell she pities me. To be the woman pushed down, forgotten by time and love. The world demands everything and offers nothing in return. Your prison is the never-ending list of expectations and silence. Your tomb is decorated with all you never achieved. The crypt is the floorboards and packed dirt. I feel myself choking, and I force my way out of the dream like ripping reality like paper.

Monsters have wormed their way into my precious dreams. They throttle the joy and take and take with a viscous, entitled grin I can hardly bare. They snake their poison into my freedoms and watch all I have crafted wither and die with a sick belief that they own what I have made. They drink up the blood between our legs, the milk from the chest and pick their teeth with our ribs and ask for *seconds*. A greedy, blubbering nonsense spills from their mouth upon our protest like the wail of a babe. Was this world not made for you? A world built on loud voices, aggression and to take and take until the next best thing comes.

The dream is broken and I am but memory and stone returned to the earth. The farmhouse, the diner, and the sun lounge are gone. All of it becomes nothing more than the fading wisp of a snuffed candle.

In the depths of darkness, between time and shadow, I awaken. The scientists and their soldiers watch me from behind the glass. Their trigger fingers twitches, a primal instinct urging them to fight. To try and flee. The Plexiglass between us may as well be tissue paper. The collar around my neck weighs heavy, and I am cold and very alone.

A voice, attempting to sound gentle, crackles out of the speaker installed in my little cave.

'Since you're awake, we wanted to run some further tests. Is this okay with you?' His voice is a little foggy. He probably fell asleep at his desk again. I drag my fingers over the cold stone and shrug. They approach me like a swarm of locusts. The soldiers keep the sights of their rifles trained on my limp form, and He examines me with an indifference half-heartedly covered up with a pale smile.

My dreams have slipped through my fingers like sand and without them, the isolation is more than I can withstand. I take his face into my hands and there is such fear in them that for a moment in all the time I have been a prisoner in this place, I feel something.

'Your tests are for nothing. For all the monsters in the world, I am just a spider in the woods.'

His beard is rough against my palm, his hazel eyes wide, and then, he takes his last breath. The collar pressed against my flesh breaks and falls to the floor and I am weightless as the night sky. The soldiers and the scientists stand. The blood in their bodies has turned to stone. In the fluorescent light of my prison, I become more. They are statues, reaching up to me, fingers desperate to touch me. But they are obsidian now.

Above, above, above.

I break through the earth, the roots. I push and push amid a tangle of thorns, I feel daylight spill across my back.

Here in the sun, thorns in my skin, I take my first breath of fresh air in a body that is my own.

4

Stockings

Sofia Chapman

The stockings I wore in the winter
got muddy and lost in the snow.
The stockings I wore in the springtime
were sparkly, fragrant, aglow.

Take stock of your things in the autumn;
spend time with your friend, not your foe.
Throw heed to the wind in the summer.
Hang the stockings, they can all go.

5

The Hollow

Arwen Verdnik

This is how I remember it:

A brother and sister stood in the sun, so close that their noses were almost touching. Like a bizarre reflection, the peaks and troughs of their faces protruded into the green negative space. They whispered words only for each other, and the delight on their faces reverberated like sound in the gap between their mirror-image profiles. Light caught the edges of their brown hair and the blonde tips of their eyelashes. Behind them were leaves, sprouts, and tendrils of edible things, blooming from every corner of the garden. Narrow veins of red bricks, half buried in the mulch, ran between the stems, where to the perpetual dismay of our adults, bare feet caught stray dirt, and carried it onto the grass, up the stairs, and into the house. The light, and the way it struck their hair, and how close they stood then. These are the things that sketch them before me, like they are really there. These are the things I always remember.

I didn't know her yet, which is maybe why they looked so similar, why she seemed so much like a scrambled combination of the features that I had begun to know in him. Spacey teeth and buried accents met me from all sides as the twins made a circle around me, joining hands and spinning, laughing madly. In my dizziness the two might have been one face, a strange division of one person that I only halfway knew. I never make friends quickly, but it was her familiarity – the looks and habits that I'd already known in him – that made me feel so comfortable. She was open and honest with everyone she knew, if only after a few short encounters. So when I'd confuse the two, refer to a secret that I'd only confided in the other, or when I misremembered who had told which story, I didn't feel embarrassed. She never made me feel embarrassed. When she wandered into a dream, or a thought, or a fantasy where I knew she didn't belong, she walked just like he did, so maybe it was okay that she was there. Or maybe it was him after all. Or neither and both – but that strange, spinning, blurry face that laughed on the grass and welcomed me like a new friend and an old friend all at once.

When this young tadpole group of ours had started to grow legs – tiny stubs that stretched the edges of our shared amphibian skin – we began to wriggle onto land. We spent time together outside the dome of our parents' sight, sustained long conversations with words we thought we understood, and began to know things about each other that our adults never had. Charlie and Caroline told me how they'd lit a small fire in the garden one night. When the twins' parents had turned out the lights, they'd stolen into the darkness, pockets heavy with matches, newspaper, and the fruits of a week's preparation. At the edge of the veggie patch, they'd made a tiny flame, stoking it with herbs that they'd collected and dried, making a column of smoke that rose lazily into the sky – their effort to touch the Gods. I can picture them so clearly, tiny figures dancing in the quivering yellow light, small hands teasing the edge of the smoke, young voices calling the names of every God they knew, trying to infuse that smoke with a part of themselves. The part that still believed in magic and was waiting to be proved correct, the part we all knew our adults lacked. Caroline knew so much about the Gods. About magic, spells, rituals, and the tiny fairy-lives that she said took place all around us, just out of sight. In the deepest part of every flower, the underside of your shoelace that never sees the sun, and in the tiny, perfect holes of special sticks you can find on days when you are very lucky, real magic was waiting to be brushed awake.

It wasn't long before we three – Charlie, Caroline, and I – had invented and refined our favourite game, *the hollow*. We spent our days capering in the thin strip of bush by the canal behind the twins' house, building, collecting, defending, and going to war. The hollow was an untame place, webbed with vines and knee-high undergrowth that blocked our movement, and frustrated our desires to run and jump and leap through the trees like wild things. The shrubs were mighty mountain ash, the drainpipes rivers, and the edge of the canal a jutting cliff, plummeting down into an expanse as vast as the sky, and as dangerous as the sea.

The hollow was always under threat, we had to remind ourselves. Enemies flanked our kingdom at every border, so we had to be ready to defend ourselves from the sudden but inevitable attacks, always looming at the edge of our home. We collected weapons and practised our fighting most days, lacing the borders of our land with sharpened spears for the times we had to abandon our lookouts. I preferred to build things, I didn't like to fight. While the twins clashed sticks and strung their bows with kitchen twine I liked to make mobiles. Strips of stringy bark made an excellent cord for suspending twigs, leaves, and stones from the canopy. My favourite held one of those special sticks, a grey disk of wood with a perfect circular hole all the way through. Charlie said it was a window made by fairies.

'They ward off evil, don't they?' Caroline asked.

'I don't know,' I said, touching the jumble of twigs and bark still limp and incomplete in my lap.

'Charlie will agree with me – don't talismans ward off evil?'

'They certainly do,' Charlie said, touching his hand to the mobile, the warmth of his fingers pressing through the leaf onto my leg.

'Just as well,' Caroline said, sniffing something in the air. When she closed her eyes, her eyelashes were flush against her cheeks, long and dark and trembling.

The mobiles worked for a while. I hung them at every bush-door, every gap in the foliage that grew thick around our favourite clearings. They required constant maintenance. When they were thrown down by the weather and scattered on the ground, I rushed to restore them, to maintain the dome of safety that held everything important. When we passed through a bush-door, a mobile over our heads, everything was okay. There may have been enemies outside, but inside we were safe. Inside, every day was the same, and when the sunlight fell through the young, green leaves, the hollow glowed from the inside out. And so did I.

But it must not have been enough. Sometimes the twins would lock eyes when we spoke about the hollow, and fill the air with energy and meaning in their joint gaze, like there was something they were hiding from me. In times like these, passing between their faces was a beam of understanding I could feel but never touch, a strange creature that only showed itself exactly when it wanted to. One day the twins encircled me, and caught me in that beam, and told me something true. There was a presence in the garden, a cruel and evil *winch*. I had heard the word before, but wasn't sure exactly where. When the twins shared this with me, that something wicked that had lodged itself in our safest place, I felt a lurch in my stomach – my own tiny winch, twisting, churning, and spreading.

'What is it?' I asked, my voice low and fast.

'An ancient evil.' Caroline said.

'It is older than the seasons,' Charlie said, 'and like the seasons it returns, and there's nothing you can do to stop it.'

'What are we going to do?' I asked.

'We have to kill it,' Caroline said, her face hard with a determination I'd never seen before.

'We can't stop it returning, but while it's young, we have a chance to destroy it,' Charlie agreed.

'It's alive?' I asked.

'Look around,' Caroline said, 'everything is alive.'

We took a few days to prepare for what would be our greatest challenge. I spent those days keeping my hands busy, building talismans, desperate to confine the darkness while I still could. Charlie and Caroline sparred for longer and with more urgency, readying themselves for the day we would confront this *winch*. They were the ones who had seen it, who knew the nature of its evil, and through the desperation with which they duelled, seemed to understand what it would cost to destroy it.

The evening came. Charlie had decided that it would be best to fight the winch during the new moon, when he said its power was thinner, and the world was less transformed by otherworldly influences. When the sky was dark, we slipped through the garden to the stretch of bush that separated their house from the canal. The water in the canal was high and slow, sliding silently along its concrete trench, a brown pulsating intestine. Its presence was immutable, pressing in on our hollow when it should have felt far away. This *winch* had already ground down the borders of the hollow, thinned out the protective shell that made our special place what it was.

We stepped slowly over the sandy floor. Dry twigs and leaves pressed into the soft, childish soles of our bare feet, whispering but not cracking, preserving the eerie quiet like we had planned. Charlie led the way. It was only I who hadn't yet seen this winch, and my outward breaths trembled like breeze as I followed the twins deep into the hollow. I began to hear a sound, a rasping, rhythmic sound ahead of us. High pitched and winding, it was coming from deep in the bushes. It was slight but also loud, as if some tiny thing were forcing all its strength into that call – that persistent, eldritch call. We all stopped, standing close, holding each other at arm's length in a small triangle. Charlie and Caroline seemed steady and alert, and I forced myself to look strong like they were, pressing air through a tiny circle in my lips, breathing through a fairy door. They were each looking at me.

'Are you ready?' Caroline whispered, her dark grey eyes pressing into mine.

I nodded.

Charlie placed his spear in my hand.

It felt so coarse and hard, the splintering bark rough on my skin. I felt the weight of it, a weight I hadn't expected to carry. I looked into Charlie's eyes, then back at Caroline's. I was warm between their bodies, spellbound.

'You're the one who keeps the evil away. You're our talisman,' Charlie said.

I had been chosen. Charlie and Caroline separated, and pressed me forward, gently, slowly, unmistakably. I stepped, and when their hands slipped from me, I felt light enough to drift into the dark, moonless sky.

'Don't come back until it's dead.'

I followed the sound of the winch. It was strange, a persisting moan that grew loud and soft and loud again, as if spinning ever closer in an arc. I knew I was near, that the sound was coming from just ahead, from a hole in the earth. One more step and I would see over the edge, down into the deep.

The way I remember it, the edge of the hole was caked with brown fur, a tangle of matted hair that had been soaked by rain and partway dried again. It drooped like a dying weed, clinging to the fleshy walls of a long, dark throat belonging to a creature bigger than any I could name. In the centre of the hole was a bald, faceless thing. With every streak of the winch's moan, it pulsated, a ripple of dark blue and purple surging in a band beneath its translucent, pink skin – an exhalation from that black windpipe that stretched down forever. I think this was the first time I understood a word that the twins liked to use: eternal. I shuffled closer, and its call became desperate, ripping and catching. I couldn't help but think that it was calling to someone. Someone that missed it. Someone lost.

I raised Charlie's spear, which seemed so small against the depthless hole. I would wait ten seconds, ten winding calls, and no longer. The small pink thing continued to scream when I forced the spear down. Its call became a cry that caught and gurgled as if through water. I closed my eyes and struck until there was silence, I can't recall how many times. I tried to pull the spear away, but the winch's soft body had stuck on the end. Maybe the twins would be angry if I left it, but I had done as they asked. They were safe now. And *I* had saved them.

A deep relief bore down on me as I returned to them, just like they had said it would. I truly could feel the evil lifting from around us, the dread and worry peeling away, drifting upwards in flakes like backwards snow. We slept in the hollow that night, and for many nights afterwards, dragging a tarp and sleeping bags out to a small clearing, surrounded by leaves above and below, huddled together and breathing in time.

Adrift among those nights beneath the stars is this. A perfect memory. Not perfect because it is clear, but perfect in another way. Only the palest of dawn lights had touched the sky when I felt a hand on my shoulder, and someone kneeling beside me. I could tell by the mess of curls, and the earthy smell surrounding me that it was one of the twins.

'Are you awake?' they asked. In answer I lifted my arm, opening myself to them. We held each other for a moment.

'Let's go get married,' they said.

'Okay.'

We clasped hands, their firm grip pressing the splinters deeper into my palm, hardened with blood and swelling as we raced through the bush containing our laughter. It was too dark to see their face, but mine ached with smiling. They stopped us at the edge of the canal, which was almost invisible in the moonless twilight.

'I love you,' I said.

'I love you,' they said.

'I've loved you forever. I *will* love you forever.'

'Do you swear it on the hollow?'

'I do.'

They kissed me – a quick, fleshy kiss that was broken with laughter and trembling as we struggled to find each other's lips in the dark. I know from memory that our feet were bare – we agreed when we set out that evening that bare feet would be the quietest, that we could come and go like breaths of wind, without disturbing whatever night-things filled the darkness. But at the same time, in my memory, there's a softness to the ground. The edge of the canal was only dry weeds and cracked concrete, but in that infant dawn, every time I remember it, we may as well have walked across a bridge of sleep.

It's a funny thing, that night. A darkness so complete it obscured the face of the person I supposedly knew best. After all my summer days were spent in watching the twins together, the way their lips made words, and the way they pushed air through the gaps in their teeth, the way they each spoke with their hands, I hadn't known the person right in front of me. The person who had led me by the hand along the jutting edge, the steepest cliff in our lives, so gently that I can't recall the feel of the ground.

Then there's the winch. The hazy web that holds that night together. Our reason for being out there. Clouded in moonless night-time, I never have been able to see it clearly, and never been able to describe to anyone else what had happened. What I had done. If I had expressed it, tried to press the memory into words, I knew it would dissolve – that what had been a summer cloud would falter in the wind, scattering into wisps that my adult hands would never be able to catch. And yet some things are always clear. The way they looked when I first saw them together. The light in their hair, and tiny glimpse of the entire world between their faces. How similar their profiles looked. The garden around them. That strange, friendly face I knew and didn't know. A face I swore I would love forever. A face I would never be able to refuse.

6

Dorada (Golden Hour)

Ahimsa Timoteo Bodhrán

Each year becomes difficult
for Granddaughter.   for Grandmother.
Always difficult, Earth Day is.
We gather here, look out,
take in the darkness, ponder
what
might have been.   could be again.
My tota   Tatarabuela
had such clear
memories
of Earth.
I   Abuela
left when
only a small child.
I helped my own   She helped her own
grandmother
carry plants aboard
for the gardens
and our own
quarters.
White Pine
still grows,
differently in space.   she always says.

The branches grow
differently.
Helixed.
Curvilinear.
Even with a-gravity.
As if hugging itself.
Still,
we are beautiful.   they are beautiful.
And the sun,
the way it breaks
through each branch.
She loves that.
Dawn and dusks,
her favourite time.
The Golden Hour.   Hora de oro.
Last light
before we see it again
tomorrow.
The way it fills the atrium,
reaches towards the light,
and the carbon we share,
it pulls each of us together.
She tells me
she tends the tree
the way she tends me.
It's why me
and our first ship
have the same name.
Esperanza.
Why this year
she gave me seedling.
Each bonsai we keep.

Shipwreck

Lucy Connelly

Cold sea winds rip at
the enduring shrubbery
of a hardened coast

dig your fingers into the rocky shelves
fingernails tearing and bloody as you
fight for a place on land.

rhythmic pounding of cold water on salty rocks
mussels and shells part your waterlogged skin
your blood wicked away by living water

a life worth living they say
is one of being torn on salt-etched rocks
shredded by a ceaseless surging

where is your fight?
lift your numb arms
your ghostly limbs

crawl on your knees
let the wind chill and frost bite
birds circle and wish for blood

with the ocean lapping at your trembling heels
singing its old song
the bittersweet promise of release

no one will forgive you
if for a moment
you let yourself slip down to where you crawled from

the lulling cry of siren waters
and a life of glassy eyes and
seaweed binding you

to a silent seafloor
a miserable wreck
who couldn't break the surface.

In the Absence of Time

Merav Fima

What a way to celebrate our last Valentine's Day together: Émile and I crying as we tightly hold each other in our arms in the small sterile stairwell of the Hôtel-Dieu Hospital, our chests rising and falling in cadence with our cries. Who will he embrace at this time next year? Will he find somebody to replace me or will he remain lonely and loyal after I'm gone? I honestly can't say which I would prefer.

We've just come out of Dr. Bélisle's office. 'Please sit down,' he said, pointing to the two plastic chairs on the opposite side of his desk. His face was as blank as his white gown; there was no trace of either sympathy or hope and he appeared completely oblivious to our inner turmoil. He must have done this a thousand times already.

Émile pulled one of the chairs out for me and I sat down with a sigh that quickly turned into a dry chest cough, the same cough that has been plaguing me these past few months. He then sat down next to me. Putting his right arm around my shoulders, he entwined the fingers of his left hand with mine. The softness and warmth of his brown cashmere scarf comforted me, as did the distinct scent of his cologne that I loved so much; but I felt my entire body shivering when a drop of melting snow slid from the sleeve of Émile's puffy down coat and landed in the palm of my hand.

The eminent doctor avoided eye contact as he flipped through the files on his desk. Meanwhile, I scanned the framed certificates lining the white wall behind him, interspersed with diagrams of the respiratory system and reproductions of Claude Monet's *Waterlilies*. At least he's got good taste in art, I thought to myself, and he seems competent enough with all those specialisations. He finally pulled my thick file from the bottom of the pile. 'Berkson, correct?' I nodded. Opening the light-brown cardboard cover, he leafed through the pages, licking his fingers to facilitate the turning of the pages and uttering 'uh-uh' from time to time. He suddenly shut the file and stiffly straightened his back. He looked first at Émile and then at me through his thick lenses supported by greening golden frames, unsure on whom to focus his gaze. He finally decided to look down at his hands, clasped together on the desk.

'I'm afraid that the results of the biopsy are much worse than I had estimated based on your lung x-ray. The cancer is very advanced and inoperable. You've got three to five months to live.' My husband tightened his hold of me and leaned toward me, closing the gap between our chairs. A tear cascaded down his cheek and I wiped it dry with the tip of my finger. I didn't know how to react to the news, but I felt another coughing fit coming on.

Three to five months, that's ninety to a hundred and fifty days and a maximum of three-thousand six-hundred hours. That means that by July I will cease to exist and will never see another autumn foliage atop Mount Royal, will not meet my niece's baby and will not attend the huge Emily Carr retrospective I had been looking forward to at the National Gallery in Ottawa. Every day that passes brings my end closer, each breath I take may be my last. Each time I go to bed it is another eight hours wasted, eight hours in which I could visit with a friend, read a novel, prepare a paper for publication and, above all, discover more of the world's wonders.

I am not yet fifty; will I make it to my birthday at the end of May? There are so many things I still want to do before I die; will I manage to complete them all? I haven't yet enjoyed all the beautiful sights that the world has to offer and haven't experienced much adventure; I haven't read all the books on my shelf, I haven't yet been to Australia or Iceland, I've never skydived or tasted frog legs, and I still don't know how to read music. Why was I condemned to such a short life? Did I do something wrong? Is it because I abandoned my parents' religious observance? Is it because I married a gentile or because I chose not to have kids? Or perhaps because I adore images and worship artists? No, I don't believe in divine retribution. So why me?

The doctor went on and on about the different therapies and medications available to lessen the pain caused by my chronic cough, but emphasised that none of it could extend my life and would undoubtedly have disagreeable side effects. I hardly heard any of it. I looked out the window at the ice-covered branches and studied the singular patterns of the snowflakes adhering to the windowpane.

I couldn't believe that my own body had betrayed me: my body that should have been my shield, my shrine. How could my own body destroy itself? Why did it allow those malignant cells to develop and spread? And why did I not feel any symptoms when it would still have been possible to cure the disease? I looked down at my body and examined my hands, the only limbs not covered in textile on this frigid winter day. Externally, my body still appeared intact, but on the inside, it was completely ravaged.

We were about to walk out of the doctor's office hand in hand, one foot already out the door, our coats draped over our shoulders and our scarves perched unevenly around our necks, when the doctor said, 'you'd better quit working and take it easy.' But I am currently teaching three courses at the university and there are two and a half months left until the end of the semester. I can't abandon my students at this point and can't burden them with my troubles. They won't even notice that I'm ill; I'll continue to deliver my lectures with as much energy as I can muster. Besides, what would I do alone at home all day long? At least at the university I meet with cheerful young people still unaware of the sorrows of life, hear their laughter and laugh with them. And the best part is that I get to share with them my favourite artworks and witness the glimmer in their eyes when they, too, come to comprehend their value. There is nothing more satisfying than getting others to admire the things you love. If I cannot continue to celebrate life and art in all its forms, I am determined to train as many people as possible to do so in my place. Yes, that would be the best use of my time, of the little time I have left on this earth. I could spend the last months of my life travelling or watching television, but I prefer to devote my time to my students and to the artists I admire. There is no reason why I should suddenly stop loving to do what I've always loved doing or why my priorities should now change.

If I were to illustrate my current state of mind, what would my painting look like? It would be abstract, I am sure, with drips of black paint in every direction, as in a Jackson Pollock canvas, or perhaps it would be all blue, as in the earlier works of Pablo Picasso's career, or maybe it would resemble Edvard Munch's *The Scream* in its bright, explosive colours. But I have never made a painting in my entire adult life and never will.

I don't want special treatment. All I want is for my last months to unfold as normally as possible. And what is more normal on a Valentine's Day than to kiss, cry and share a good meal?

I rise from the step, grab Émile's hand, pull him up and race him down the hospital stairs. I then drag him into the fancy restaurant across the street where we go each year on this day. There is no time to waste crying.

9

Round and Round
the Garden

Carmel Bird

For thirty years now I have run an arborist and landscaping business. The name was invented by my daughter Clementine, when she was about five, and it grew on me. *Mr Lop-Lop.* You'd have to say it's memorable. Our real name is Brown, and when I'm not being Mr Lop-Lop I'm known as Capability. Actually, it's *James* Brown. But some of my work is more than capable, if I do say so myself. The local Council often give me quite big projects.

My wife Madeleine and I have always loved gardens, but we have never really taken the time to make one of our own. She runs the giftshop along-side *Mr Lop-Lop*. Her business is *Round and Round*, specialising in garden ornaments and all sorts of teddy bears. She and her friend Nell used to make tartan jackets for the bears. The little ceramic ones are quite popular – people sometimes like to put them on graves. Clem works for both of us, doing the books and so forth. She always says Madeleine has a great sense of artistic design. She's probably right.

But you don't want to hear about all that. Down to business, right?

The other day Clem said did I remember Gerry Godkin. How could I forget? But why was she asking. Well, she said, it seems his wife Lily has died and he wants us to help re-organise the garden. In her memory? I said, and Clem said yes, something like that. Grief takes people in different ways – I've seen that. Before I called Gerry back, I checked the records to make sure I was dealing with the same Godkins. Same address. OK. I had sometimes wondered what became of the Godkins. Some clients you get to know. With others you just have to fill in the blanks.

This was the thing. Lily, a small pale nervous woman in her fifties, rang me about twenty-five years earlier and asked me to go round there and give her a quote. Scruffy trackies and a grey apron. Turned out she wanted the whole garden cleared. You will bring the stump-muncher, wont' you? She was particularly insistent about the stump-muncher. I told her that added a lot to the cost, but she was determined. There was even a kind of defiance in her mood. I don't want a single thing left in the ground, she said. So, I quoted, she agreed, the boys and I razed the block – mainly lots of mature native trees and shrubs set out in fairly random rows.

It took three full days to get everything done.

I can't wait till Gerry sees it, Lily said, rather slowly and with a kind of dreamy emphasis. He's away on Council business. It's a surprise. I asked if they would be needing any landscape design or so, but she said no that wasn't the idea. I kind of wondered what the idea was, but I didn't give it a lot of thought. She paid me upfront in cash. A bit unusual, Madeleine said, taking the words right out of my mouth as usual, and we went out for dinner at the Willy Wombat Grill. Madeleine was wearing a bright green scarf she'd just knitted. It didn't really suit her, but what would I know?

Two days later I was in the grotty local pub after work, and at the other end of the bar there was an old bloke drinking himself stupid. Not unusual. He was glued to the tv watching the races with a kind of glazed stare. But when a neighbour called out to me, he suddenly came to life. He jerked his head and stared at me for a bit, and then he staggered over, half a schooner in his fist. You Mr Lop-Lop? he said. I nodded. Then he held up his glass and slowly poured the beer over my head. Good job, Mr Stump-Muncher, he half-shouted, half-growled. People turned around then looked away. I wiped the beer out of my eyes, and two other blokes took the drunk by the elbows and hustled him out into the night.

That was Gerry Godkin, the barman said. His wife has left him. He's pretty cut up about it. Well, I could see that. Then the barman put two and two together and said to me – I guess you were involved in the thing with the garden, eh Lop-Lop? Gerry planted it all out when they bought the house. It meant a lot to him. More than she did, actually, we reckon. Well, they say she's gone to live with her sister, and he's by himself in the house with no trees. No children. People thought they were a devoted couple. Funny business. You wouldn't think it to look at him, but he works for the Council, got some kind of office in the Town Hall.

That was the last I heard of any of it for all these years. A few times I drove past the house. Early on the garden just sat there like a landscape on the moon with the neat weatherboard marooned in the middle and a Hill's Hoist always empty, as far as I could tell. It was one of those blank, sad houses with what Madeleine calls 'no personality'. For a long time the place was just a wilderness – weeds everywhere. Then later the whole place was rank with weeds. Next somebody more or less cleaned it up and planted a whole regiment of hideous iceberg roses. Well, it was a fashion in those days. I can't stand them. And Madeleine is with me on that of course. I thought maybe somebody else was living there, but one time as I was driving past, I saw the woman – older, but with the trackies and the apron and so forth same as Lily's – making quite a good job of pruning the roses.

But as I say, the other day, Clem said Gerry Godkin, same phone, same address, wanted me to call him. Was he going to apologise for the baptism by beer? Not likely. Did I even want to speak to him? Guess what, curiosity got the better of me.

Gerry Godkin?

Speaking.

James Brown here.

Yes. Thank you for calling back. I have a job for you.

He gave me the same address from twenty-five years back and I went round. He met me at the gate wearing thick grey gardening gloves, a kind of wild triumphant look in his eyes. A thin stream of dark blood trickled down his cheek.

About half the rose bushes had been violently yanked out of the ground and were lying all over the place a bit like bodies on a battlefield. Not that I've seen a battlefield. Gerry waved his arms in a vigorous gesture, and I reckon those mad eyes were practically popping out of his head.

Now I want all this cleared. Really cleared. You can do it? I think you cleared this garden once, a few years ago, Mr Lop-Lop, he said.

I believe I did.

In the long look that followed, neither of us mentioned the beer.

Well, I would like you to give a repeat performance. As soon as possible. You will possibly need to bring your stump muncher to deal with a couple of very old tree stumps you seem to have missed last time. I will be away for a week. Just send the invoice when you're done.

When I got back to the office I told Clem what had happened, and she said she had just read in the local paper that Lily Godkin's funeral was private and no flowers by request. It only took me a day to do the clearing. Actually, I hate working with rose bushes. They can fling themselves at any accidentally exposed bit of flesh and really dig their teeth in.

That would have been the end of it, except that Madeleine's friend Nell of the tartan jackets died and we went to the burial in the new natural section of the old cemetery. Instead of headstones and stone slabs they bury you under a native tree, and the graves are heaped with stuff like twigs and feathers and toys and pebbles and photos and flags with poetry on them and so forth. You guessed it – as we wandered at random between the mounds under the straggly trees, we came to Lily Godkin's grave. And there, half-buried in the leaf litter was a framed photograph of the weatherboard house as it stood in a garden full of native trees and grasses. Stamped on the severe metal frame were the words 'In Memory of Lily Godkin'. But the strange sad thing was this – resting on the ground beside the photo there was a small ceramic teddy bear with a faded blue satin ribbon round its neck. I sometimes think I will never understand people.

10

Oh, the Places You Won't Go

(A Reworking of Dr Seuss)

Angela Jones

Oh, the places you won't go
after 7pm at night
not because you're paranoid
or live a life in fright
but you've walked the streets of Brunswick, Northbridge and Redfern
and have decided that you'd rather live, than end up in an urn.

Oh, the places you won't go
not even to the pub?
but it is only 5 mins away
you'll be alright love
but you were followed 3 weeks ago down that very road
you hid inside the laundromat and caught an Uber home

Oh, the places you won't go
so, you're taking back the night?
that's a bunch of femmo crap
everything's alright
us men aren't all like that, it's only a crazy few
we don't need you ladies telling us to mind our crew

Oh, the places you won't go
I didn't get a raise in pay
even though Tom and Laz
showed me the other day
that they're paid higher for doing the same work
HR denied just it, treated me like I'm the jerk

Oh, the places you won't go
you're in line for a promotion
8 years of solid service
it's all been put in motion
but the director he's best mates with the new recruit
sorry kid, it's now his role, maybe next time wear a suit

Oh, the places you won't go
to actually voice your mind
every instance that you go to speak
your voice is maligned
it's you who is the problem, change your tone and your behaviour
you set the men against you, they'll not be your saviour

Oh, the places you won't go
even with brains and strong shoes
you cannot steer yourself
in any direction that you choose
you are not the one who gets to decide
the places where you'll linger or if you're left outside.

Oh, the places you won't go
you didn't realise when you were 10
that you operate in a time and space
in a world that belongs to men
and if you voice your dismay, you will certainly hear a hiss
for we have now gone back in time to the place where feminists –
are hated more than terrorists
and must really hate those men
because why else would they be so vocal
look at all we've given them?

Oh, the places you won't go, it's all inside your head
less pay, less jobs, less human rights… or that you may wind up dead.
try to walk the not-so-good street
at night to work or home
and when you walk these places
you don't need to feel alone
because someone is always watching, we'd like you all to know
there'll always be someone to ensure, there's places you won't go

11

Respect vs Woe

Deborah Lee

The word defiant is not on my lips.
Not in my breath.
It is not in the air.
It is nowhere to be found.

Defeat has gnawed my fingernails.
Crept into my ribcage.
Wrenched my gut sideways.
Heart-stricken, my hands just fists.

The supreme court?
Roe now just means caviar.
Privilege. Capitalism excess.
The loss, egregious. Unfathomable.

The supreme court?
Wade might as well mean
waylaid. Devastation.
Annihilation. Desecration.

Bodily autonomy?
Black Lives Matter?
How can I laugh?
Can I ever laugh again?

Roe vs Wade.
No more laughter.
No more joy.
Terror. Tears.

Respect vs Woe.
Fears for the future. What is
this dystopia? What once
was thought to be paranoia?

Religion vs Women.
How can any woman believe
this is for the children?
For life? For love?

I praise my barren and
deformed womb. I thank
goodness for disease and
invisible illness.

I wish it could be
passed to others.
I wish, I wish,
I wish.

But I do not hope.
I whisper.
I cry. I hug.
I sigh with loss.

I would hold all women
wounded by this court.
Wounded by rape culture.
Wounded by patriarchy.

Woe, women, woe.

No

Kellie Tori

It's your favourite word now
You're little but stand tall
Wearing your belly out front with pride
You've just learnt its sound
How to shape your fledgling mouth
round its power

Its simplicity is revolutionary

No.

No Mum.

Your arm stretched
wrist flexed
Body emphasising, always
I hear you

No.

It comes from your boots

No.

It comes with ease

No.

It comes with glee

Teach me, please
How to not flinch at its promise
How to reverse the entrenchment of its implicit impoliteness
Could you, please?

Would you mind?

Teach me to say no to the friend who took too much
to the boy turned man who wouldn't leave
and wouldn't let me let myself
to anyone who asked
the world

Please teach me

No Mum.

Ok. Thank you.

13

Awake at 2am

Paris Rosemont

She woke up
    in a changed world
stripped time-
    traveller flung
into a different century
losing her bearings in a
    wild
wild west she no longer re-
cognised as home. No longer safe
for her to venture into pine need-
led woods alone free-
    dom plucked bare as her in-
vogue bush as she is fucked
over by the patriarchy.

Start running, *Little Red* –
you and your homegirl hussies
from the hood are now mis-
understood second-class citizens
brought to your knees
in order to please

Commanders
who will force you to breed
the fruits of their wicked seed
        unless
you choose to swallow
this dystopia.

You burrow underground
fleeing to find alternate routes
gambling with crude currency –
head or tail? It will cost you
        either way;
handsome price to pay
by desperate women held at ransom.

Carve out sin like Jack
        o' lanterns scooping
out mucky seeds coat
hanger wire scraping away future
bullets dodged before they get too
        comfortable in their lodgings;
womb with a view to over-
population. Come, grab your popcorn
for a lap dance from Miss Pop-
ular! Pop one out for the mother,
pop another for the father
and pop one for that lucky bastard of a cunt-
ry!
        Pop...
                pop...
                        pop...
                                STOP!

From under the cloak
of a bleak black sky tiny stars blink
away disbelief as they hear the call to arms.
It is time.

And all of a sudden
      the sky illuminates
with the brilliance
of a thousand angry eyes
glittering fierce as diamonds.

14

Phoenix Rising

Charlotte Romeo

The blade grew heavy in Nieve's trembling palms, the metallic stench of blood stinging her nostrils as it spread through the throne room.

Nieve had never seen so much as a speck of dust littered upon these floors.

Now, King Graysel's blood stained her reflection in the once-grey marble, tainting the stone of his kingdom one last time.

She had done it. The girl had finally snapped. Now, the King of Ceylwa lay lifeless on the swirling tiles before her as she peeled her dagger from his side, admiring the glistening runes along its hilt as she turned it over in her hands.

Nieve always knew she would be the one to kill the King. Not once had the idea repulsed her; not after all she'd endured. But she couldn't help the thickness rising in her throat, the sudden weakness in her unsteady fingers as the blade slipped from her grasp, the sharp clatter of silver echoing against the walls.

The King was truly gone. At last, she had slaughtered the overbearing tyrant they had called a leader; and as tradition held, his title would be passed to her – the one to overthrow him. A saviour in every right but blood; a ruler in every inch but desire.

Graysel had never been kind to her – had only allowed his growing obsession with the land's magic to drive him to insanity. An unlikely blessing for Nieve, however, the bastard-born girl left to fade away on the King's forest floor. Where she was raised not to parade her body, and smile politely to potential suitors as women were expected, but where she found refuge in learning how to fight – how to *survive* – in more ways than just physical.

Where her education lacked, her primal instinct flourished. Where others' uncertainty grew, she thrived with the certitude that pulsed beneath her skin.

Those carefully honed skills are what granted her the opportunity so rarely offered to females – a sinister yet necessary step towards the future she dreamed of creating. In the King's madness, her clarity would thrive, she had told him; as part of his Kingdom, her unrivalled knowledge of his lands would grant him greater wealth than he could ever dream of holding within his grasp.

But despite his years of practice in the fields of secrecy and lies –

He had believed her in a heartbeat.

Desperation of any sort does that to one's judgement, Nieve supposed; like calls to like in any measure of folly. So, it was her innocent smiles that yielded her flickers of insight thought lost upon dull ears. Her perfectly timed naivety granted her slivers of knowledge heard by none other than the King's entourage.

She'd had no intentions of keeping it that way.

Drawing her mind from the trance, Nieve felt the corners of her lips tilt in a smirk as she lifted her blade once more, slowly wiping the steel clean over her sodden pants. She dragged each glorious moment out as she felt the eyes of the room glide with her swift hands, observing every breath she took before them. Felt the fear shift between them as the blade sparkled under the chandelier's watch, as though it had never been unsheathed. Such a lovely contrast to its fatal creation, produced for nothing more than malice if she so dared will it.

The King believed he had added a blunt dagger to his polished collection when Nieve had arrived.

None of them noticed she had become the most lethal weapon of them all. Cleaving the guards apart from the inside of their units; pitting them against one another sentinel by sentinel.

And for the loyalty the King saw she provided their lands, he had granted her a fraction of her own magic to wield – deemed harmless by ordinary standards, but deadly by her own.

Granted her the same magic that drove her dagger to make that precise, clean cut through his abdomen, even from where she stood angled behind his throne. The same magic that she now felt shudder through the land as it set itself free from the King's bound chains when his soul finally escaped his body.

With a flick of her wrist, a flash of glorious flame appeared in Nieve's palm, the unrestrained hues of orange and scarlet warmth that she had longed to behold seeping through her veins. With another swift whirl, the King's body had vanished, a flare of light the only sign he ever truly existed.

Despite the silence spanning the room, Nieve raised her head to the surrounding crowd and allowed her cheeks to lift in a slight smile. Allowed her back to turn on the King's fleeting ashes, for her body to rise on steady feet as she held her head high to the people gathered around the room.

None of them dared release a breath at the raging phoenix before them.

Because that is what Nieve had become over the years – a perfectly honed blade hidden behind sheaths of dazzling gowns and faint cherry blushes that now stood blazing where they once knelt before their King.

The first noble to fall to one knee was Count Ericon of Kaera. Nieve held his gaze as he lowered himself; returned the sly smile he gave only for her as his eyes gleamed with approval.

The next, Lord Carequon. He held his crown of gold to his chest, his eyes dancing as they glistened with his own newly restored light – the gift of the stars, the moon, and the vast expanse of darkness spanning between.

Count Starlon, Lady Visling, Duke Wetchington. One by one, the citizens of Ceylwa knelt before their new Queen. With each passing moment, the hints of shock guttered out, an air of anticipation kindling in its wake.

Nieve knew the continent had been starved of freedom under King Graysel's rule – she had not realised that they would delight in his demise so openly. So *soon*.

She welcomed the heat that crackled in her eyes, her hair, now. As the boldest nobles dared glance above their brows and beheld the blazing crown that beckoned above her own.

A brighter future – that is the portrait Nieve presented to the people bowing for her. The image of hope, of faith, of how their world may stand if she were the one leading it. If she were the one to *change* it.

Just as she knew the decision she would make with the King, she knew the decision she now had to make as their Queen. She knew that she could take on this Kingdom, the burdens left behind by generations of heartless beasts. She could help Ceylwa *thrive* if she let her heart dream wildly enough.

And Nieve knew exactly how she wished to do so.

In her first and only rule as their leader, Nieve relished in the gasps that flitted through the room as her sparks settled on the throne behind her.

As the citizens of Ceylwa watched their throne burn to cinders.

'Do not kneel for my crown,' her unyielding voice ordered the room, the air coarse with reservation. With the lift of her hand, they rose on hesitant feet. 'I do not wish to rule, and I do not wish to be Queen.' With that, the burning crown above her hair evaporated.

'I was left to rot in the forests of this kingdom.' She glanced to Lady Gale, the poor woman who provided food and comfort for years after she found her withering away amongst the leaves. 'I was left to fight my way to this throne because of who I am and where I was born.' To Librarian Delor, the man who taught her that knowledge is a tool more powerful than any weapon she could hold in her palms; that her mind would be her curse and her blessing, and shifted the hilt to arm her with the latter.

'I was left to stand before that King and grovel at his feet as he so wished me.' A final glance to Nathan, the kind male who offered her half his loaf of bread, when half was all he had remaining.

'I know what it is to starve. I know what it is to mourn a life that you have never lived, in my lost time and in lives long before that. I do not wish to see such struggle prevail in our world for lives longer.

'Centuries of torment died with King Graysel. With his death shall his legacy die, too. I have no wishes as your Queen now; I have no desire to stand before you all and see you beg as I was once forced to.

'All I ask is for this new world to be brighter than the last – that this is a world ruled not by one but *all* of us. One where freedom and peace prevail in our lands – where wrongdoings are righted not by force, but love. One where slaves and nobles alike are freed from the grasp of the long-standing systems that are only dragging us further apart from our whole.

'I do not wish to be Queen, and I do not wish to rule.' She did not mind the stinging that settled in her eyes as she met each gaze in the room. She knew theirs shone all the same.

'But I do wish,' she continued, her grin growing as she let the long-held words flow freely from her chest, 'for this new Ceylwa to spark the start of a new people. That our new nation is fuelled by *your* hearts – that you will all be part of our *country's* beating heart, and that throne is never rebuilt again – is the only request I have for all of you.'

She saw the words sink in as her eyes scanned the room. Every soul knew what those words meant: no other could lead this kingdom unless allocated the line of ruling by Nieve herself. Or by force, as Nieve had done to the King, but she knew that would be of no concern, by the number of people beaming at her now.

The people she now gazed out towards with her first genuine smile; the people who shared her same vision of building a world that is better than the one the King left behind.

And while Nieve's voice may not have faltered, she had loosened her hold on the tightening in her chest, the squeezing of her heart against her ribcage as she felt the salty trail of teardrops sliding down her features.

For the first time in her life, Nieve did not mind the tears that fell – the tears she knew were not a sign of weakness, but a sign of the battle righteously won. For the first time, she did not mind basking in the grin she shared with these people – a feeling she had not allowed herself to imagine for fear of losing it in the depths of the King's brutal reign.

For she would not let a ruler restrain her joy any longer; would not let a ruler suppress the hope of the people she had fought beside – the people she had fought *for* – all this time. The ones who knelt before the King unafraid; the ones who dared hold her stare when she waltzed into the Kingdom with muddy footprints and a shredded tunic that first morning.

The people who so willingly bowed to her as their new Queen, when all she really wanted was the lack of any Queen at all.

As the sea of bodies parted before her, Nieve grasped the hands of the family she had created, the pockets of light that guided her through the depths of this dark kingdom. She smiled for her brothers and sisters, for Delor and Nathan and Gale as they walked hand in hand, side by side, into the rays of light ahead of the Kingdom's archway. Into the light of the brighter world waiting for them beyond.

Nieve would not let another moment of suffering overwhelm this continent; would not let feats deemed impossible limit her or her companions a single breath longer.

For this was the beginning of the new world she had dreamed of in that forest as a child – the new Ceylwa that she had dreamed of forging when she held nothing but broken hope and a shattered heart in her hands.

And with her final steps away from the Kingdom that had controlled their lives for centuries, Nieve allowed herself to truly savour the warmth of the sun's heat dancing upon her shining cheeks as she strode towards the brighter world they were crafting.

Because they were flame.

They were defiant.

They were the brighter future they had all dreamed of creating.

The future that began in that forest when a single heart had dared to dream.

15

Are You a Writer?

Koraly Dimitriadis

If you are a writer,
you may need
to ask yourself

am I a puppet or
a writer?

Puppet has become
the new hipster,
as the literati chink
their glasses,
the panellists
keep their seats warm
for the next round,
pull down their pants,
ready to hand out new badges
to the most critically acclaimed kissers

If you are a writer, ask yourself:
Do you write what you really think?
Do you sound like everybody else?
Do you try to mould and shape-shift
present yourself like a present to
the mainstream?

Mainstream left
or the mainstream right
it's really the same thing,
clinging to the safety
of solidarity,
for argument's sake

Sure, there's safety in numbers
We all want to get paid
Best to pick a side
& stick to it
But ask yourself,
are you perpetuating problems
to stay clicked into the clique
for the glory of retweets?

Both the left and the right,
they don't want change,
they just want to stay
stuck in their ways
I wonder sometimes:
Do I live inside fairy-tale snow-globe
because I hope for change?

They'll try to burn you
at the stake from both sides
if you go out on a limb
Be fearless, be bold
You may think the cost is too great,
but if we all don't rise up and speak,
say what we really think,
humanity will have to
foot the silence
instead

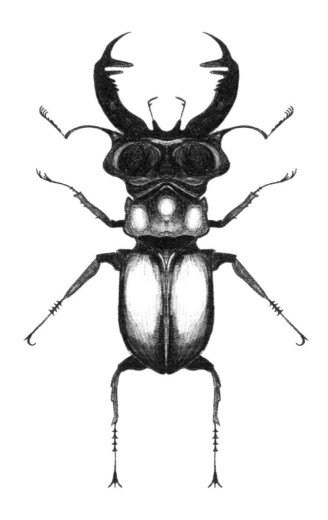

16

Chimaera

Elena Disilvestro

Outside, the howling of the wind tore through the trees. The window trembled in its wake, at the mercy of the branches and the pelting rain. Struggling against the billowing curtains, Clementine reached forward, grasping the latch and slamming the panes of glass shut with one final heave. She slumped onto her seat, head lolling forward into the shivering embrace of her hands. Gingerly, she pressed the tips of her fingers to the skin of her eyelids in a feeble attempt to quell the ache behind. At least now, with the raucous on-slaught being drowned out by the glass, she could hear herself think.

The letter sat crumpled in front of her, scarlet ink drawing her like a moth to flame. By now she could recite it, yet she continued to read over it, over and over until the words on the parchment muddled together and lost all sense. A bleeding splotch waited for her attention at the bottom where the rain had smeared the writing. Reaching forward, she smoothed out the creases with her palms and lifted the letter once more to the candlelight.

Dearest Clementine Ackworth,

The Arcane Committee delights in welcoming you to the 93rd biannual State Examination.

As a state researcher for the Arcane Department of Occult Organisms and Artificial Lifeforms, you are legally mandated to attend and present your latest thesis to the committee. Your presentation must match, or surpass, the quality of your previous entries to the State Examination, and it must include a live-viewing of an arcane-made lifeform never before seen by the committee. Failure to adhere to these requirements, or any others listed under Section 798 of the official Arcane Examination Rulebook (AER), will result in the immediate termination of your contract and retrieval of any and all magical artefacts under your ownership.

We wish to remind you of our collective and unanimous admiration of your last entry, it stands to this day as one of the most impressive and useful entries the examination chamber has ever received.

Your examination is scheduled for the 6th of June, it shall take place inside your respective department's primary dungeon. We extend an invitation to your newly appointed assistant as well; we know how helpful he could be to you.

Sincerely,
Alfred Burton
Chief Examiner

June 6th. One week.

Instinctively, her eyes drifted to the shelves along the back wall of her brewery. The rotten wood seemed to bend almost to the point of fracture under the weight of what it carried. Rows upon rows of jars lined every single one, each of them corked and filled with a thick, gelatinous fluid. Suspended within were countless organisms. A tri-headed canine, a winged newt, an ordinary beetle. Each specimen laid there festering, staring unseeingly into the room.

A timid creak stole her attention. As her head swivelled towards the source, her eyes met his. He was all limbs, a lanky frame engulfed by a frayed knit jumper. The cowlick at the back of his skull tickled the ceiling as he bowed his head to enter the room, feathery strands falling across his eyes. Hunched and unsteady, he waddled over to her, tray in hand.

The tray landed softly on her table in a tinkling choir of metal and porcelain. Just as softly came his voice.

'Thought you might be hungry.'

Clementine allowed herself to survey the offering. Freshly brewed honey-suckle tea with a slice of orange cake, both served in ornate crockery, the dainty kind made to sit within the haven of a display cabinet. She lifted her gaze once more and met his eyes for a second time. They were a light grey, irises flitting all over the room. His hands trembled at his sides, grasping at the hem of his jumper to dry out the sweat of his palms. He reminded her of a hummingbird.

'Thank you, you always know how to help.' She allowed a smile to settle over her features, the gesture felt foreign but regardless of how odd it must have appeared, it was enough, for he glowed in response and scuttled out of the room. She waited for the soft thump of the closing door before she settled back into her thoughts.

It had been a month since the department had appointed him to her. Apparently, it was customary to provide high ranking researchers with assistants. This seemed all well and good, for the state usually provided veteran academics, not eager young men. Had Clementine been more sceptical of her department, she might have read into the sly smiles of her co-workers as they remarked how *helpful* he would be to her and her *situation*. She might have interpreted allusions to her age and whispers of her 'too-long wait' to refer to matters outside of academia. Clementine might even have felt troubled by Alfred extending him an invitation, considering the typical union necessary for such a formality. Perhaps she was sceptical enough. Perhaps it made no difference.

Once again, her gaze found the scarlet ink.

June 6th, one week.

She turned and scrunched her nose at her festering shelves, and when she found nothing worth anything, as she knew she would, she turned to her cauldron.

Guided by the pounding of the rain, she set the fire ablaze for the fifth time that evening. Again, she opened the occult texts that littered her workspace and, again, she found the relevant pages. With the gurgling of her brew and the thundering of the tempest, Clementine began the process anew.

Half a litre of water, five-hundred grams of carbon, twice that much of salt and half that of sulphur. Then the ammonia and the silicon, then crushed obsidian and agate followed by the liquid of three pomegranate seeds...

Mindlessly she followed her recipe, mindlessly she retraced her steps one by one until they met their end. As the mixture boiled and spilled over the edge, scorching the tarnished floor below, Clementine turned to her shelf once more to pick which jar to waste. She chose the beetle, for she could always venture to the forest and catch more. Tearing the cork from its place atop the jar, Clementine tipped the contents onto the cauldron's tumultuous sludge. She watched it consume the beetle with a vacant stare and, after she stirred it seventeen times, deigned to glance down at the fruit of her labour.

Where she expected a charred and valueless ooze, she instead found a beetle. Furrowing her brows, she reached down and took a hold of it. Holding it up to the flickering candle, Clementine inspected the insect with newfound interest. It was a stag beetle, black and shiny, utterly identical to the one she dumped into the mixture. But that beetle should've broken down, at the very least it should've burned. She turned it over and over on her palm until she was certain that she could draw it from memory and, to her utmost disappointment, found absolutely nothing of note. With clenched teeth and one final sigh, she chucked the insect onto her desk.

Soundlessly, she left for bed.

* * *

The sun found the wreckage of the night's downpour.

Broken branches and bent trunks obscured the view out of the brewery window, casting misshapen shadows across the wooden floorboards. Clementine stood without purpose in the middle of the room and stared without seeing at the books on the floor, allowing her mind to drift further and further away. Her self-imposed punishment soon came to an end as he shuffled into the room. Once again, his hair tickled the ceiling as he bent awkwardly to fit into her space. Once again, he placed adorned silverware and pastries on top of her desk. Once again, he murmured some inconsequential remark, and once again she smiled and replied: 'Thank you, you always know how to help.'

As the door closed, announcing his retreat, Clementine contemplated the contents of today's plate. Hibiscus tea and a cream slice. For a second she considered leaving it there, refusing the offering. Then she thought of the letter, and of Alfred's invitation, and her co-workers' snide remarks. She put the fork to her mouth.

As she chewed her third bite, she noticed movement out of the corner of her eye. Scurrying across her tabletop there it was: the stag beetle. Warily she lowered her fork. It had been dead the last time she saw it, of that, she was sure. She felt uneasy as she watched its legs scamper across the uneven surface. As she began reaching out toward it, the beetle found a spider in its path.

Before she could reach it, the stag beetle opened a mouth that it should not have, a mouth lined with jagged teeth which it sunk deep into the arachnid's flesh with a sickening crunch. A mouth with which it chewed the spider's body, limb by limb, gnawing as it swallowed until it was all gone.

For a few seconds there was nothing. Just her and the beetle and unbroken silence. And then the beetle convulsed. A leg sprouted out of its belly, spraying the desk with a green ichor. Then three more followed on the same side, then four on the other. Each leg made it jolt in pain; each leg soaked the wood in ichor. The beetle screeched in agony as it tore itself apart and sewed itself back together. Its body sputtered in a revolting display as it mutated, and then, as quickly as it began, it was over.

Her hand hung rigidly in mid-air, frozen halfway through its approach to grab the being that was most certainly not a stag beetle. She stared breathlessly as it turned to her with its new form, as it began to advance toward her, skittish and unsure. Clementine did not dare blink, paralysed, as she stared at it crawl. Where originally it had had the six thin legs of a beetle, now it held those in tandem with the eight thick, tufted and curved legs of its prey. It moved with the same disturbing dexterity of a spider, with its beetle legs scuttling desperately to keep haste. It reached her hand quicker than it could've before its meal and, feebly, brushed her fingers with one arachnid limb. Clementine remained still as it did, as it gained courage and clambered her outstretched fingers until it began an ascent up her hand, up her arm, until it reached her shoulder and met her, eye to eye.

Outside, the rain had returned. It fell in soft applause as Clementine smiled down at her muse. A quiet, incredulous laugh fell from her lips, and she let herself be engulfed by it for a moment. For the first time in weeks, she felt the smile reach her eyes. For the first time in even longer, she felt her chest lighten, free of a load she was unaware she had. She stared down at her marvellous creation. It was miraculous, a beastly conglomerate with a ravenous little mouth. She reached for it wondrously with one tentative fingertip and to her delight, it leaned to her touch without fright. She could not help her glee as she caressed the smooth curve of its body and admired her work. Her *chimaera*.

With nimble fingers she held its body and watched it squirm in confusion; gently she placed it atop the desk and watched it scuttle, vying for her attention. She felt lighter, hopeful, but she was not yet deluded. Yes, this was a fantastic start. No, this was not enough.

With sudden urgency she stood, alarming the poor little chimaera. Apologetically, Clementine caressed its gleaming shell, murmuring a promise of soon return, and then scampered out the door.

The faint patter of rain followed her through the forest as she left her cabin, petrichor permeating the air. Twigs snapped under her footsteps as she hurried beneath the canopy, eyes darting, searching frantically for her prey. She found it by its delicate song, a sweet melody accompanied by the buzzing flutter of wings. The hummingbird weaved through the bushes, joyous under the safety of the foliage, until it reached Clementine and perched atop her outstretched limb. Oblivious and innocent, it waited for the sugar water she would usually bring, and instead found the steady prison of her grip. It squeaked and ruffled its feathers in a futile attempt to break free, but too late, for her feet were already marching her back to her stead. Back through the canopy, back through the drizzling rain, through the open cabin door and down the stairs. She was still savouring her victory when the sound of shattering porcelain broke her daze.

Staggering, she glanced down at the crockery she had trampled on her tread. The splintered fragments of a frail teacup were sprinkled over the wood in a puddle of warm honeyed liquid. Her other foot had trodden over the dessert, strawberry cheesecake, her favourite. The door to the brewery stood ajar, held in place by the fallen tray, and from within came the noise. An echoing crunch, a sinewy chew, the splintering of something akin to bone.

The hummingbird flew out of her loosened grip.

It took three steps to reach the tray, two more to look through the gap of the door, and through the measly opening she saw it. It was animalistic, a grotesque amalgamation contorted over its meal. It masticated with human teeth, blood dripping down onto the woollen jumper below its claws. Each chew mutated it, each swallow convulsed its frame. A puddle of ichor formed beneath it, growing with each new leg, fingernail and hair. A row of beetle legs lined its spine, like spikes down its alabaster skin. It stood on eight humanoid legs, curved and arranged like those of its first hunt, but now fleshed and adorned with knees and toes. It heaved, famished, as it devoured some more, its face obstructed by a curtain of greasy locks, broken only by a cowlick at the back of its skull. As if aware of her stare, it grew still, and with perturbing caution, turned to her.

Its body bobbed unsteadily as its mangled frame advanced to the door. It nibbled on a finger as it reached her feet and, expectantly, it waited for her. Hesitantly, it presented its head, an offering. When she stood motionless, it prodded her leg, and when she remained still even then, it made a whining noise, yearning for her approval. In desperation, it met her stare, and, with light grey eyes, it contorted its mouth around a word.

'Hun...gry?'

It was barely a voice, more of a hoarse croak. But it was enough. Gently, she extended her hand, and, with great delight, the chimaera nuzzled into her palm. She felt the ichor stain her skin.

'You always know how to help.'

Exegesis

Chimaera marks my venture into prose. Inspired by the narrative ambiguity of 'The Summer People' and free indirect style of 'The Story of an Hour', it is a gory amalgamation of the fear and loss of autonomy I often near when confronted with the chance that I might one day reach a point where my gender becomes a barrier to my career. Clementine's plight, struggling against an otherwise unanimously male workforce as it attempts to prioritise her lack of romantic or familial life over her profession, echoes a struggle I hear women face perennially. Through a fantastical, escapist lens I attempt to conjure a reality in which she may, literally, eat away at these societal barricades; a fantasy not granted to a myriad of women outside of the page.

The free, indirect style employed by 'The Story of an Hour' allows for an exploration of womanhood as perceived by the protagonist, whilst maintaining its third-person perspective, a technique I wished to mirror. Within Chopin's text, the narrative often adopts the diction we expect from Mrs Mallard, allowing a glimpse into her inner turmoil, subsequent exhilarating delight, and momentary acquisition of power. Within my own work, I first attempt to provide a glimpse into the opposite, into Clementine's loss of self-government as the narrator ponders that 'Perhaps she was sceptical enough. Perhaps it made no difference.' Throughout the story, instances of free, indirect style harken back to this power imbalance, but they also allow for unnervingly joyous responses to morbid stimuli. In much the same way that Mrs Mallard does not 'stop to ask if it were or were not a monstrous joy' (Chopin 164), Clementine allows herself to be engulfed by laughter at the grotesque sight of the chimaera mutilating itself. Although both women are experiencing gruesome tales, they are also being granted autonomy, a defiant gift which to them surpasses whatever mutation or death lies before them.

Throughout the narrative, I also wished to maintain a certain level of ambiguity. The vagueness in the ending of 'The Summer People' greatly inspired me in this regard. Both the lack of clarity regarding the true intention of the town's folk, and the haunting wait which ends the tale, leave the reality of the situation up to interpretation. I attempted to leave my ending similarly vague. At the end of the tale, does Clementine feel fulfilled? Is she content with this outcome, with the devouring of her assistant as it provides her with an organism for her examination and an escape from her dilemma? Or is she attempting to appease the beast that now resides in her home, fearful of her own creation and awaiting the day where she too becomes a meal? Is she truly free, or has she merely overcome a harmless representative of her struggle? I know my answer to these questions, but, hopefully, it is not so obviously framed in the text, so that a reader may form their own conclusion.

References

Chopin, Kate. 'The Story of an Hour'. *The Storm and Other Stories*. Edited by Per Seyersted. New York: The Feminist Press, 1974.

Jackson, Shirley. 'The Summer People'. *Dark Tales*. New York: Penguin, 2017.

Upon Hearing You Are No Longer Loved By the One You Love

Cameron Semmens

Those liquid screams
pressing at your eyeballs –
suck them in!
Keeping sucking.
Suck in all the air you can –
it's an airbag for your heart.
Embrace the suckiness of this moment.
It sucks!
They suck!
You suck.
Suck it in.
Suck it up.
Don't be a victim of their sucking.
Suck first.
Suck on your own terms.
Suck like you always planned to suck.
Fill up the emptiness
with your spit
and your rage
and your rotten mourning breath.
Blow up like a puffer fish –
swell in defence.

Hold back the tears.
Hold them back.
Hold on.
Hold it.
Hold it in.
'Cause you need to listen
– you really need to listen –
before the earth-quaking sobs
shake the monuments of your life
from their crumbling plinths.
Just suck it all in
'cause you'll want to remember,
you'll *really* want to remember
what they have to say.
Let me tell you
– from experience –
you'll want to remember *exactly*
what they have to say
and *how* they say it.
And the pauses –
those evil spaces,
those vacant lots,
those gaping holes –
you'll want to remember *exactly*
where the pauses were.
So, listen, and keep listening,
'til *they* walk away
or *you* walk away
until you both turn
and walk away.

And later, *later*…

when you have the space,
by yourself,
or by a friend,
or buying ice-cream
scream! scream! scream!
Through face
and future *scream!*
Through windscreens
and castle walls *scream!*
Through sick cultures
and circling vultures *scream!*
Through Why's
and How's
and eyes
and vows
scream! scream! scream!

The Rain's Lament

Melanie Hutchinson

It was my fault. I held on too tight.

The endless rain started falling the night my son was born. It was gentle in the beginning, almost soothing as I cradled my baby; captivated by the miracle of life as I stared at him breathing soft new breaths.

In. Out.

His chest moving, gently.

Up.

Down.

At first the rain brought welcome relief from the scorching heat and uncompromising humidity. All living creatures felt the reprieve as the rain painted colour back into our sepia landscape. Festively curated garden beds decorated median strips and roadsides for kilometres. Most ornately festooned was the main highway, adorned with *melati* flowers and bougainvilleas, stretching from the airport to the city. Lanes of traffic whizzed past the floral kaleidoscope with chaotic purpose. Diesel infused plumes of progress rose high into the atmosphere. Off the main thoroughfares the interior was alive with industry. Street vendors jostled each other, competing for the afternoon commuter trade. People travelled from far and wide to visit our picture-perfect world.

We were grateful. So was my garden. In response to the nourishing cloud-burst it bloomed, coming alive with colour – vibrant reds, pinks, oranges, purples, and greens. My garden flourished in those early days of my son's life.

But the endless rain had its own ambition, refusing to give way to the dry season. The perpetual monsoon continued, steadily overflowing the reservoirs, bloating the rivers, engorging waterways as hastily constructed storm water drains burst, transforming roads into rivers.

It wasn't long before our back garden became a watery grave for my red hibiscus, pink moon orchids and fiery *dadap merah* bushes. Plastic toys floated with nowhere to go except as directed by the muddy water. My son's swing dangled from the tallest of the frangipani trees, its yellow plastic seat already drowned. In the evening, the frangipanis saturated the night air with their hopeful fragrance.

I grieved for the garden I had carefully cultivated. My sanctuary. Later, a space for my son to play and grow. He turned six last week and plays with his toys inside the house now. He hasn't yet learned to swim.

A sudden surge of the tide. Our boat lurches. Still tethered to the water-logged dock by a worn, flimsy rope. Our only lifeline. It just needs to hold on a short while longer. Dark clouds gather overhead. Distressing the already weeping sky. Shadowy harbingers of the thing we had silently agreed not to discuss. As the light drains from the day, the hour of our departure inches closer.

We follow instructions.

We sit.

Silent.

A frozen tableau in an innocuous looking wooden vessel as it rocks in lilting cadence with the growing swell.

Hiding in plain sight.

Waiting.

And the rain continues its perpetual lament.

It started slowly at first. The sinking of our cities.

The land is subsiding, declared environmental experts.

Into the sea.

But no-one believed them.

It is impossible for our mighty cities to sink. Look how big and strong they are, pronounced the developers.

Our skyscrapers are among the grandest in the world. They can't possibly sink, we proudly boasted.

Something needs to be done, the environmentalists counselled.

Before it's too late.

But their warnings went unheeded, and the environmentalists left. Not long before the rain began. The rest of us stayed. Resolute, with faith in our superiority. Development and progress competed to keep pace with technology. Ours was a modern world. Impressive skyscrapers were built. State-of-the-art, priapic, they were filled with cutting-edge entertainment, high-end shopping malls, Michelin star restaurants, bowling alleys, hanging gardens, indoor playgrounds and lavish accommodation.

We are the masters of our environment, we declared, with the hubris of a people accustomed to the luxury of modern conveniences.

The swell burgeons as we sail. Each salty undulation of water expanding into a surging leviathan. Foamy tentacles grasp at our flimsy vessel as it lurches from one heaving, rolling, watery colossus to the next. Our numb, raw, wet fingers cling to whatever is within reach. Our lives cleaved within our tense grips.

Wave after endless wave.

We are soaked through. Basted in a mix of sea-spray and rain. I can feel my fingers slipping, losing their grip on the edge of the boat as it lurches upwards, carried high above the ocean by another heaving wave. I hold my breath, waiting for the moment the boat is released.

D

o

w

n.

Luuuurch.

It is only a moment. A simple reflexive action. I squeeze my son's tiny wrist as, yet another surge engulfs us, wrapping us in a terrifying blanket of salty sea. He yelps. A tiny, pitiful sound. Filled with terror. I clutch him closer, smothering his mouth with my right hand.

We have a plan, the government said. *Be patient.*

But as we waited, the sea continued to hungrily devour our land. Province by province. Aided by the endless rain.

Don't worry, the officials said. *Land sometimes sinks. Especially tiny islands. It will all turn out well in the end.*

So we waited.

Trusting.

Patient.

Obedient.

The greedy sea continued to feast. Dining on nearby, low-lying islands and atolls. We were told not to panic. The government would build special walls to contain the sea's hunger. But the rain was unrelenting; a perpetual flow swelling the sea's appetite.

Java started to disappear under the salty sea. Bali was swallowed in one gluttonous gulp, leaving just the tip of Mount Agung poking its ashen nose out of the island's watery grave. In the distance, Mount Raung's unsubmerged head gazed silently back at Mount Agung.

Where will the tourists go? Economists asked.

Don't worry, the officials said. *We will find a new place for the tourists. They are vital to our economy. We will build a better Bali. Far from the water.*

And so, the tourists continued to visit, many unaware that Bali was once known for its beautiful beaches and coastline.

More special walls were built. But they were too porous for the endless rain which eroded these purpose-built structures from the top as the ravenous sea ate its way through their bottom. When Jakarta began its final descent into the sea's watery bowels, all of Java was on the brink of being devoured.

Not to worry, the officials said.

We will build a new Jakarta. It will be even more prosperous. They crowed.

We will build the world's greatest smart city. A green city connected by 'The Cloud' to give citizens a better quality of life. A city that will be the environmental envy of the world.

All citizens have a duty to stay, they resolved.

To rebuild our great country.

For the economy.

Evacuations are against the law, came the decree.

Who will populate the new smart cities if everyone is allowed to leave? The government reasoned.

The pre-school where I taught was abandoned when the classrooms swallowed too much water and the buildings drowned.

Don't be afraid, the officials told me.

You don't need to work. Soon you will be living in a smart city. They explained. *It will be your duty to make more babies with your husband. Brothers and sisters for your son. Children for the future.*

My husband agreed. It was for the best. He had been relocated to build the new smart city with the other engineers and town planners and special experts. I was to join him when the first housing sector had been completed.

I waited with the others in our watery homes. Watching the rising lake lap hungrily at our doorstep as the foundations of our weather-worn house slid steadily into the sodden soil.

It won't be long, my husband assured me. *The new city will be ready soon and we will live together as before, only better. We will be richly rewarded for our ingenuity. We will have a good life*, he promised.

I wanted to believe him and resisted the daily temptation to leave.

I will wait, I promised.

He faithfully continued his work. Designing. Building. Assuring our future. The city would be magnificent. His face beamed as he told me of their progress during our daily calls.

Well done, I encouraged.

Soon you can come, he promised. *Very soon. We will have a modern home where we will grow our family.*

Still the endless rain fell. Some days a mere drizzle, other days torrential. But it never stopped. Feeding the lake in our backyard until it joined forces with the hungry sea, encroaching closer and higher. Consuming the ground floor entirely. Forcing us to move into the upper level of our house. I worried about it getting into the electricals. The life glowing in my cell phone's charge gave me comfort.

Soon it would be too late to leave.

One day my husband didn't call. When I called him, his phone rang out. I left a message.

Don't worry, my friends and neighbours said. *He'll call tomorrow. He's just busy today.*

Eventually we realised that those remaining had lost contact with the ones building the smart city.

We waited.

When the waiting became too much, talk inevitably turned to leaving.

Where would we go? Asked one of us.

Australia. There's no rain there, replied another.

Australia is always dry now agreed another.

Too dry, not enough drinking water for everyone, complained one who chose to stay behind.

The sea has swallowed Sydney too, and many of the coastal cities, someone else said.

We will head for one of the new smart cities, built on higher ground, like Mount Gambier, Toowoomba, Herberton, or even the former Snowy Mountains, someone who knew Australia suggested.

How will we get there? We asked.

The airports are flooded. And those that aren't are closed to international travel while the smart cities get built, declared another.

Someone announced they had a boat that could take us.

What if we get caught?

We left in secret. The captain's power hung dark and low. A ruthless, cumulonimbus. His word was law. No exceptions.

There are unmarked patrol boats that stalk the waters surrounding Australia, the captain said. *They are known as Ghost Patrols, undetectable to modern radar technology. They haunt the seas, seeking out boats like ours, alert to the faintest sounds, their thermal heat detectors intuit the slightest change in thermal radiation. If they sense us, they will kill us.* He paused, pointedly stroking his gun.

If anybody makes a sound, or does anything to draw attention to us, I will silence them.

A metal cylinder was attached to the barrel. I had only ever seen a gun once before, when they knocked on our door to escort my husband to the site of the new smart city, with the other 'needed' citizens.

Fear had already muted our voices.

We nodded obediently.

P

U

D

o

w

n.

*Luuuur*c*h*.

My stomach churns to the rhythm of the storm's fury. I look up as the captain turns his head in our direction. The metallic barrel of his gun glints in the darkness as he silences the accidental noise that caught his attention. Another wave towers above the boat. There's no time to think as it grips our flimsy vessel, wrapping its foamy, curling hands around us. My son falls limp in my lap. I hold him close, smelling the sweet, sweaty smell that is distinctly his, holding him tightly as sea spray washes his blood over us both.

The rain persists its relentless deluge as our journey continues. Each wave a surge closer to our destination. Soon we will be on dry land.

Safe.

In a land with no rain.

My son.

I want to hold him forever, but my aching body deadens under his weight. Exhausted, my eyelids heavy, I cling to his slippery, stiffening form, squeezing him close. Until an unfeeling, hungry wave sweeps my lifeless son from my reluctant arms, gathering him into the cold, salty embrace of the dark swell.

I watch my hope disappear into the watery abyss and will the hungry sea to swallow me too. Yet its cruel appetite seems sated at last. Its salty tentacles leave me to my fate in the flimsy boat, carrying us closer and closer towards dry land as the endless rain continues.

Persistent.

Rhythmic.

Falling on my skin. Pooling around my feet and ankles as the boat fills with water.

The captain directs us to use the buckets under our seats to bail the rising water from the tilting vessel. With cold, numb arms, we obey.

Slosh. Toss.

Slosh. Toss.

We throw water overboard as fast as we can. I hear a terrified scream as someone loses their balance and follows their bucket over the side of the boat. The muted crack of the captain's gun silences the rest of us into a tableau of fear.

Slosh. Toss.

Someone behind me resumes bailing the water out with a steady rhythm.

Slosh. Toss.

The percussive cadence breaks our freeze and one by one the rest of us join in. Avoiding eye contact. Silently focussed on the task of staying afloat.

The storm's anger is easing, appeased by the accidental sacrifice of my only child and the stranger who keeps him company in their vast, brackish grave. The endless rain continues, but more lightly, as the waves recede. Our boat rolls over the now-gentle swell, rocking in rhythmic consolation.

A flickering of light catches my eye. Looking up I see curlews flying purposefully overhead.

Land is near. They sing to each other as they begin their descent, before flying out of sight.

Land is near.

19

She

Ibtisam Shahbaz

she was a child of beauty
with her father's wisdom
and mother's heart
a childhood filled with love
the infant of the treetops
worn carpet stains that spelled love
filled with candlelight and honey

but as she grew
the world transformed
laughter in the garden became the lonely cry of a swing
she used to scream so vividly
now all the notes have married silence
doubt whispers across the ceiling
drowning amongst the crisp paint of white
she
a flailing spirit
clawing at the corners
the peel of paint crumbling only to reveal another wall
her heart a fragrant teacup in one's hand
holding a breath that never left
hidden behind the faintest of smiles
loneliness stood her only companion
a stillness
running from the game they tried to paint as life

now
she undergoes a rebirth
staring at the lost and found
and the crown misery took from her
one day
to fall back into her hands
I will rise again.
Perhaps,
I already am.
and they shall see a woman of fervour
with softness and strength intertwined
She'll leave them wondering who she ever was
A force of might and love
A woman to behold
A daughter who loved
and a mother to her own being.

20

Redrawing the Line

Jane Downing

The director of the anime was irascible, but known to get results. 'Girls, girls, girls,' he bellowed, 'get into your positions. We only have the Scottish castle until morning. And I'm talking to you too Kitty.'

Kitty stood up from her crouch at the bottom of the frame. Her cheeks glowed pinkly as a pleasing contrast to her green hair. 'But Director, Sir, my pinafore is missing its final touches.'

She'd been in the middle of consulting the illustrator, who reached up to point out the problem. The director squinted at the offending piece of clothing and between the two men, they were able to verify Kitty's concerns.

'Okay. Take five,' the director decided.

The other two girls, Missy and Pretty, jumped out of the anime frame and preened in front of a mirror. They twirled and flounced and their hair swung freely from the points beneath butterfly ribbons, and their skirts wheeled just high enough to hint at lacey knickers but no more. The bows at the backs of *their* pinafores were as gorgeously plump and perfect as those on top of Disney Christmas presents.

'It's just your bow,' Pretty shouted back up at Kitty who was last to climb out of the frame. Kitty had to move more slowly so her pinny wouldn't fall forward without her. Her breasts bounced as she landed on the studio floor, and the line of her cleavage continued to jiggle until she put her hand up to stop it. And in so doing, she flattened the frill around the pinafore's bib, in some places smudging it beyond recognition.

'Oh heavens above, I need even more help. A touch up at the front as well,' she cried.

Missy and Pretty settled in two of the high-backed banqueting chairs that were being designed for a coming scene while Kitty remained standing under the ministrations of a junior illustrator.

The chairs were highly ornate in the way of occidental nobility and the same design aesthetic continued in the landscape. The three girls could only see a few key frames ahead but it was enough to make out an expanding exterior picture of rugged mountains, multiple castle turrets and coloured banners. In between these few key frames, a teacher in a flowing black gown appeared and reappeared in the classroom and corridors they'd temporarily escaped.

'It's all a bit Pigswarts,' Missy observed.

'Hog,' simpered Kitty of the kit-malfunction.

'I am not. Stop name calling,' bristled Missy. 'You dog,' she added for good measure.

'Do you know who the monster is, in this season of *Demon Dragons of Defiance*?' Pretty asked as a distraction. This sort of question usually helped to stop the bickering between her co-stars, because on some things they could rely no matter who the director was: hair of pretty pastel hue, long socks, a school room, an apocalypse – and a monster. 'This place is giving off a heavy vampire vibe,' she observed.

'A robot vampire?' Missy suggested, drawn into the guessing game.

'Godzilla!' shouted Kitty from by the mirror. She'd meant to talk in a conversational tone but the cold nub of the illustrator's pencil had touched her bosoms just as she'd opened her mouth. She looked askance at him. He kept his eyes down with a lock of black hair obscuring his expression.

'Oh no, it can't be Godzilla,' Missy disagreed and not only because she enjoyed disagreeing with Kitty over everything. 'Haven't you heard? He's got those big Hollywood gigs. He won't be back for a while.'

'Perhaps it'll be something new,' sighed Pretty.

There were guffaws all round. The illustrator and the stylists and props men scattered about the studio joined in. Anime was a world of creation: on the first day was the word and on the second the pantheon of monsters was created. And that was that. There could be no new horrors. Which was something the girls kept in mind whenever they were out of frame. The vast empty spaces beyond their closed circle of characters could send you snowblind. Some certainties were necessary.

'I'll get the colourist now,' the illustrator told Kitty once he'd stopped tickling the small of her back with his thickest black pen.

'Do you have to? The bow and the frill are white. There's no colour.' Kitty aimed for an innocent girly voice in full flirtatious plea. She didn't like the colourist. And not because she was jealous of the brown eyes he'd given Pretty while she was stuck with blue eyes which she was convinced clashed with her green hair.

'You still need white on white – all the shading you goose,' the illustrator said as he disappeared into the uniform white of the studio.

Kitty obediently stayed standing. 'The designers don't respect us,' she told her slouching sister classmates.

Orange-haired Missy widened her big Bambi-mother eyes until they were completely round like saucers. 'Respect? Have you seen your *waifu* pillow?'

'My branded merchandise sells very well, thank you very much. I'm so sexy. The fans love me,' Kitty preened.

'They only love us because they can put their own words in our mouths,' sighed Pretty. She crossed her legs daintily from their previous sprawl over the sketched banqueting chair.

'And for the other side,' smirked Missy.

'What other side?' asked Kitty, genuinely confused.

'The other side of those body-length pillows that sell so well to your fans. The side of the *waifu* where you are naked except for the flouncy bow in your tossed green hair.' Pretty explained all the details because Kitty was *so* naïve. 'Naked except for your bow, and those long white socks.'

'Naked! I didn't pose for that.'

'None of us did,' laughed Missy derisively. 'Real life is not like up there in the frames. Real guys don't drop a handy nosebleed trope to indicate to the audience they are sexually aroused. In real life they just grab the *waifu* pillow and...'

'Stop being crude.' Pretty stopped Missy full flight. 'What a man does with his legally purchased anime-decorated body-sized pillow in the privacy of his own shut-in bedroom, is his own business.' Pretty was a good actor but the others could tell she was parroting something she'd heard.

'Yuck, I feel soiled,' grimaced Kitty now that she knew.

'Like an unlaundered *waifu*?' Missy laughed.

'Next boy character who gets a nosebleed around me, I'll punch him in the face and give him something to really bleed about,' Kitty declared.

The colourist materialised behind Kitty. He was a florid fellow who could have done well to add a few contrasts to his own cheeks. He bustled up with a bouquet of brushes, some fat, some eloquently thin and some whisker fine. Kitty indicated the areas she had wardrobe issues and lifted her chin so he could work on the frill around her pinny's bib.

'Stop tickling,' she asked sweetly. She was careful not to crinkle her nose against his whiskey breath.

Missy and Pretty continued to lounge nearby, but now they were uncharacteristically silent. It wasn't only Kitty – none of them liked the colourist. He was less subtle than the illustrator, more hands-on. He went around to Kitty's back and self-importantly appraised the bow situation from various distances.

The silence was too much. 'I wish we could stay in the classroom more often and not have to go out and save the world from monsters,' Pretty said to break it. She sighed deeply as the man worked on her friend's nether regions. 'It looked like a really interesting lesson on the blackboard.'

All three girls scanned the closest key frames and the in-betweens to get the full picture of what the *sensei* was writing. An elaborate diagram explaining greenhouse gas emissions and consequences was sketched in chalk-white. 'Ah, so that's how. I'd always wondered how it worked,' Pretty said with a little bit of satisfaction.

Kitty hadn't got to read the last blackboard in the sequence, the one fully covered with drawings and words. Her concentration had been interrupted. She hissed between her teeth. 'Do you mind?' She tossed her green hair elaborately, but the colourist showed no indication he'd picked up on the symbolism of the hair-action. Her stylised defiance was nothing to him. He did not pause in his colouring. Or his straying.

Missy and Pretty tried to stay focused on the series of blackboards in the tweeners. And Kitty tried more forcefully to stop the colourist's untoward touches.

'Keep your brushes above the hemline if you don't mind.' She blushed, ready to reject his apology. Which never came.

'The illustrator wants you to fix the bow,' Kitty tried again. 'There is no reason to be…' She squealed.

The colourist finally spoke. 'Your hem needed re-colouring,' he said gruffly.

'That was not my hem,' Kitty whispered as he walked away.

Pretty, always the kindest on the set, stood up and came over. 'Are you okay?' she asked.

'It must have been a slip of the brush?' Kitty's voice quavered. They all knew it hadn't been an accidental slip because it'd happened again and again. So why was it so difficult to let themselves believe his touching was deliberate and nasty.

'You look beautiful,' Pretty told Kitty to lift her mood.

'I look exactly like you two except for my hair and eye colour,' she protested.

'Why thank you. So we're all beautiful,' smiled Missy archly, her radiant glow in full force. But this time she wasn't going to let the others be distracted. 'Which doesn't help,' she added. 'It's just not on, the way they manhandle us. Maybe we should do something about it.'

'Settle petals,' called the director. 'You're all set. Back into the frames you go.'

The petals looked at each other.

'No time to waste. Think of your fans.' He clapped smartly to get them moving.

The girls, girls, girls all immediately had the same thought about their fans. And the other side of the bed linen. Then their second thoughts were of the piles and piles of fan mail with its unadulterated adoration.

Kitty leapt up into the last frame they'd left and Missy followed. She put her hand down to help pull Pretty up. The junior illustrator put his hand on Pretty's bottom to push. He pinched hard.

Pretty turned.

'I'm only helping,' he smirked.

Pretty let herself fall back into the whitespace of the studio, her blue hair swaying as if in a gale. Kitty and Missy looked down at her from the edge of the frame. Pretty was always the one who made things right when they were feeling uncomfortable. The diplomat. The consoler.

'Up you go, slow poke,' the director boomed. 'Lickety-split, quick sticks.'

Pretty crossed her arms in front of her lacy pinafore. She looked at her friends, not at the director. Her blue hair was no longer flouncing with caricatured defiance. They had to look harder beyond stylised anime tropes to her real expression. 'Do we really have to let it go each time? Again and again?'

The director appeared not to hear her. 'Girls, girls, girls, time to take your positions.'

'How about we don't?' Pretty asked quietly.

I Am Still the Ocean

Ashleigh K. Rose

I've dressed in aquamarine
kissed the coastline shores
wore power suits of sapphire hues
spoke language of waves' roar.

Painted myself in cloud blue
to imitate the sky
misled by youthful impressions
that's what it took for acceptance in life.

I've sparkled in sunlight surfaces
and sunk into endless midnights
felt at home amongst stir and swell
and the rise and fall of tide.

Drowned cities with my tsunami
kept hope afloat with my surf
never anchored to one continent
always connected to the Earth.

For I am still the ocean
transcending chapter and age
to define me as only one of my parts
robs me of my right to change.

What Do You Yearn For?

Ibtisam Shahbaz

Music pulsing on a nerve
Constructs unidentifiable
Growing, falling, settling
Within

Break the shackles of limitations
the gold lining of their lies are but a prison
March on
To see the light fracture through its embers
Find the hope of beauty amongst the rubble of pain
Lift the clipped shards of oneself
The doubt
The hurt
The regret
The pieces we avoid,
And the ones we cower behind.
Hold them in our hands and let the discomfort bleed
Notice your reflection
Fractured faces, ideas of self
Who are you, *really*?
Hold these ruins in the palm of your writhing hands
Piece by piece
Unearth your roots of love
Fall and flourish
Until you cannot be shattered any longer.

23

Love Child

Jenny Hedley

I say you must not
like me very much you
say that must mean you hate
me you ask if you can

do something / give me
the biggest cuddle in the universe
love me to infinity and beyond
you want to know

if I love you that big
how do I say: more than life
without shifting the burden
of life on your teensy

shoulders with the muscles you make
me squeeze so I can tell you how big
they're growing so I can tell you
in ten years you will be as tall as the roof
swing me around like an action figure

I say listen to mommy but how
can I say you should not listen to mommy
when she is outside herself swimming

a well of anger / an ocean of illness / a volcano of trauma
poised and ready to explode
under slight provocation how do I explain
the order I make you keep in your room
is only to soothe the disorder in my mind

that you are the calm / the balm
caught in the fury of my own reflection

24

Pink

Tessa Martin

One

I was one when they bathed me, scrubbed me, dried and dressed me in a pastel pink jumpsuit. Doe-eyed, I gazed at a carousel of colours as plump clouds and stars hung from strings above my change table.

'Darling, girl', they whispered, as they watched me like a campfire, all sparks of orange and ruby, wrapped in pink.

Five

My favourite colour was blue, or at least that is what I would tell you. Sapphire, aqua, sky, you name it. I wore blue like a medal swinging from my neck that says *'I will be different'*.

In a line like soldiers ready to bolt when commanded, we waited for the teacher to call something that we related to.

'Run if your favourite colour is pink', he yelled.

Pink. I smiled and with my nose thrust in the air I kept my feet together like my shoelaces had been tied.

'Darling, are you going to run? all the other girls are running', he prompted.

In a moment, he lent a name to my defiance, defining exactly who I didn't want to be, *'all the other girls'*. So I crossed my arms and watched as their backs ran away from me. Shaking my head, I refused to chase them. To run barefoot with painted toenails hidden under frilly socks, to chase glitter handed girls in summer dresses. To chase strawberry bubblegum and silly little bows. Everything I longed to be, I refused to chase. I especially refused to chase pink.

Six

My aqua lunchbox sat proudly amongst the sea of pink boxes, most were glittered or sequined, sometimes both. I often had to pull my eyes away from the boxes as the sunlight danced on the rosy specks, or I might have almost wanted one.

'Darling, do you want to buy a pink lunchbox?', my dad offered in the shop aisles.

I shook my head stubbornly against his understandable expectation. I wanted to stand out amongst the girls, not to be seen as masculine, but to present as sporty and strong like the boys in blue. If I was honest, I did it for them. To be liked by the boys was to be taken seriously, it was to be accepted and made real in the world of a six year old.

'Water is blue,' I told myself. 'You like water. You like to swim. So you can like blue.' So blue was my favourite colour.

Eight

In the back seat of a rundown Falcon with a scratchy radio, a pitchy American voice came out from amongst the static.

'I'm a blond bimbo girl in a fantasy world'
'Dress me up, make it tight, I'm your dolly'
'You're my doll, rock'n'roll, feel the glamour in pink'

My legs and head shook along to the beat of the music like the limbs of a rag doll, rhythmless but free, until my sister's hand swiped the volume knob down low. She whipped her head around from the driver's seat, with the look of indignation.

'Darling, don't be like the girl in this song. Ok?', she pleaded.

'Like who?'

'Like Barbie. You don't need to be like Barbie.'

What is wrong with Barbie? I thought. But I nodded as my own blonde plastic figure began burning in my tiny hand like red coals. As I looked the doll up and down I noticed, for the first time, the pointiness of each breast and the thinness of the plastic. I tried to recall any girls I knew that looked like her, I could maybe manage two, but even they weren't so thin that they could snap in my hands if I tried.

My sister burnt one of my Barbie dolls once, in our open wood fire, to see what would happen when her body met the flames. We all watched as her plastic breasts sunk into her body and her features ran in drips down her face. Her hair caught alight like straw and her plastic body morphed into liquid beneath the coals. Dead, or at least I felt like she had died. But something fake can never really die, and that's all she was. Fake beauty that could melt under real fire. Only two women I could think of with beauty that couldn't melt, or perhaps they could, but all I knew was deep down I wanted to make that number three. To be pretty enough that all they can think to do is burn you for their own envy. But really, I would rather have blood pump through my veins and skin on my bones than be fake if it meant I would snap and burn like her.

'Don't be like Barbie' I recited, like the chorus of a song. So I let her slip through my fingers to join the rubbish beneath the seat.

Twelve

'She kicks and she scores', I screamed as my friend sent a leather pink football flying directly between the goal posts. The feeling was riveting, even for a school game. My friend thrust the bottom seam of her shirt over her head like a true soccer player. We followed suit, jogging a couple of metres across the oval in a triumphant line. A celebration we had seen the boys do excessively after every goal they scored.

But as my friends and I sat with our heads hung in the detention room, like dogs being trained, the reality was no longer a game.

'Darling girls, your bodies are different to the boys', we can't allow you to do that', the teacher told us.

When I saw the differences between us, my eyes became fixed on how we are treated so differently. I realised it isn't just in the way our atoms combined or our bodies took form. It is the way we dance differently through life, to contrary drums. We could put on the performance of our lives and still only be a man's understudy, fulfilling a complementary role. I saw that we cannot move in the freedom of our bodies, be unapologetically loud or carelessly expressive. Why, no matter how recklessly we try, can we not be treated as men?

Sixteen

I'd like to say that my feminist realisation wasn't dependent on a man. I'd rather say that I stole sunsets, shattered the moon and mixed galaxies like soup for my breakfast without a man in sight. I'd like to say I became a feminist without a man even opening his mouth but it was their words that made me:

'Darling, did you put those shorts on tight for me?'
'Darling, I'd hit that'
'Darling, why don't you bring yourself over here?'
'Darling, that ass could umpire my games anyday'

Hot tears burned down my face as I ran around the boundary of the oval. I was at work. In the span of one football game I felt the tightrope that I had balanced on so precariously my entire life, snap from beneath me. I fell into defiance of both the *'darling girl'* and the good feminist I was taught to be.

'Don't let them see you cry, don't let them win', I thought over and over until it rang in my ears, the same way it would every day of my life. The *'them'* that I set my heart against that day were not men, not the specific boys that yelled to me during that football game I umpired or the senior men who told me to get over it. It was the society that told men it was okay to talk to a 16 year old girl this way. Of course, I had always believed that women were just as capable as men, I saw no alternative to that truth. But it wasn't until I felt this injustice that awareness spread in me like black tar filling my lungs, making it hard to breathe. I had never hollered from behind the fence of an oval but I had denied women, including myself, the cool hand of womanhood.

So, with the pride of a lioness, I tightened the laces of my pink football boots and let them carry me back onto the field. And I ran and I ran, newly fearless of myself and the world's voices behind me.

Seventeen

I was angry. Not all of the time, but it hid like a shadow behind my eyes waiting for a cue to cover my face, lower my brows and ready my mouth for a fight. I expected the worst in people so they gave me exactly that. I would scream unfiltered thoughts fuelled with facts, bitter words and long quotes. But they would dissolve like sparks in the air, the only fire it ignited was in the pit of my own stomach and the blood coursing in my veins. My words never bothered anyone as much as theirs bothered me.

'*Darling, nobody listens to you when you are angry. They only want to rile you up more,*' my mother always said.

I have always wondered why we are such a source of amusement. Why do they bait us, like throwing fairy floss and popcorn at caged lions? They throw and they throw until the popcorn turns to rocks. They laugh as the rocks pound our skin, leaving marks on pink flesh. Like a game of '*watch the angry girl scramble*'. They love to watch as we are plagued with the problems in the world, even better when we point them out, like how the roar of a lion both scares and amuses a crowd. To them, I became the problem when I spoke of the problem, and I became the angry, overly emotional girl. Why is anger only deemed emotional when attached to women?

'*Don't let them win*'. It rang again in my ears, with a new meaning; don't give them a game.

Eighteen

They continued to poke, to bait and to throw rocks, never truly understanding the weight of womanhood that swung from my hips like a skirt. '*Darling, if you are such a feminist then why do you like the colour pink?*', they teased with both the intention to rouse a laugh and a hint of genuine curiosity.

Still my cheeks turned the very colour they mocked me for, as I decoded the meaning of their inquiry. What they really wanted to know was, 'if you are such a feminist then why do you allow yourself to be seen as weak?' Because to them, if I am a feminist and I want to prove that women are strong, I should adopt qualities that present me as such. To them, these qualities are inherently masculine. So they were asking me why I would choose to be so '*girly*' because, to them, to be '*girly*' is to undermine my stance that women are strong.

'I'm claiming it back', I mustered.

'From what?'

'Your notion of it.'

They smirked, of course. Bemused by my ambiguity but at least I didn't spit fire at the mention of feminism, like a dragon being awoken, as I did in the past.

But they didn't hear what I truly wished to say. What I wanted to ask them:

Have you seen a sunset? No seriously. Have you seen the way the heavens fight through the cracks in the sky at the tip of twilight? Or when, between the ticks of a clock, the heavens blush, turning skin pink and filtering the eyes? Even Vincent van Gogh's brushes have seen the beauty in the warm strokes of a sunset, attempting to replicate the greatest oil painting in the sky.

They would have laughed, I'm sure, to hear me ask if they had seen the day turn to night. It is not like a street light turning off, like a forbidden moment that no one ever really catches. No, a sunset demands to be seen, the same way the ocean frames the horizon and refuses to be ignored.

So I know the answer... you have seen a sunset.

But what I don't understand is how, then, could you see pink as anything but power?

When the sky turns shades of rose and fuchsia, nobody stops to think *'oh how frivolous and weak this sky must be'* to be pink. You mistake beauty for fakeness, but truly there is nothing more beautiful and real than a pink sunset. And that is the power of a woman.

I wanted to tell them; I wear pink to feel powerful because being a woman takes blood, sweat and tears...and yes I said blood. To deny myself a colour purely because it is feminine is to agree that femininity is something to be ashamed of, which I no longer believe. I have learnt that true feminism is to embrace femininity not fear it.

So, I will adorn myself in pink, tie it in my hair and hang it from my limbs like armour, as a sign that I will not turn away from what you call feminine. I refuse to agree with you, to agree with society, by masking myself in blue to hide my womanhood for fear of your words. Though you may continue to call us dainty, weak and superficial, I know that being a woman is not for the faint hearted. Being a woman is strength, power and beauty, all wrapped in a pink bow.

Twenty one

I will be feminine.
I will see myself in the reflection of rose tinted sunsets.
I will write love poems to the stars and make art from wildflowers. I
will be friends with women. Whether they squeal, dance or annoy. I
will care for other women.
I will chew strawberry Bubblegum between gloss painted lips. I will
stop to smell lavender on paved sidewalks and smile at children. I will
shave my legs when I feel like it or I will wear hair like jewels when I
feel like being accessorised.

Yes, sometimes I will still spit fire and fight like a raging storm. I will
still run barefoot through dust and scrape my toes on tree roots. I will
kick footballs, tear my clothes and knot my hair. I will be heard, I will
be bold, I will be powerful.

But I will dress in floral like a grandmother, in a short black skirt and a
sporting uniform. All on the same day.
I will long to walk a runway in pointy shoes and stick fragmented
pieces of magazines above my bed.
I will laugh at silly jokes until I gasp for air and my buttons
pop. I will buy a glitter lunchbox and run when they say
pink.
I will marry a man, not because he is perfect but because he is
fascinatingly different from me.
I will draw love hearts down the margins of novels.

I will wear pink until I bleed it.

Oh but I promise…
'Darling, I will still be a feminist.'

25

My Mummy Yells Like That Because

Koraly Dimitriadis

My mummy doesn't talk loud because
she's trying to be annoying
My mummy doesn't talk loud to be funny
like all the wog comedy depicts
She doesn't shout and nag
for me to do things
in an over-the-top way
to be dramatic or indifferent,
my mummy yells like that
because she's been repressed
because she's been shut down,
my mummy yells like that
because she's trying to explode out
of the box patriarchy put her in to shut her up
My mummy doesn't yell to make some
wog guy comedy writer money
so they can keep getting the gigs
while us women sit on our seats,
my mummy yells because she was shipped off
to another country to be married
when she was nineteen
so she could pop out a couple of kids
and she had no choice in the matter

My mummy yells like that,
like a loud, aggressive whine
like someone is smashing bottles over your head
because she's fucking tired
she's fucking over it
she's over fucking knowing
that Haroula down the road
is still getting bashed by her husband 20 years later
and she can't say nothing but
'ti na kanoume?'
'what can we do?'
My mummy yells because she's over it
And she can't even say it
Because she doesn't know how
She's not even aware of it
And that's why it's my job
to write this poem
& to do something
about it

26

Video Game Baby

Lilly O'Gorman

We'd decided that, for the long weekend, the baby and I would travel alone. I was standing on the footpath in front of our house watching Kyle load everything into our hatchback. A year ago, Kyle sold our second car and replaced it with an ebike. At the time, I had been happy to save money on rego and servicing, so didn't complain.

'But what if there's an emergency while I'm gone,' I said to Kyle's back. He was bent over the baby's car seat, fiddling with the buckle, re-loosening and re-tightening the straps. The baby squirmed.

'Emergency?' He stood up and stared at the seat, trying to figure out whether he'd missed a crucial harnessing step. He wasn't listening to me.

'You slip in the shower, concuss yourself,' I said. 'You leave the stove on and the house burns down.'

'I don't think the car's going to help me in either scenario. But thanks.' He grabbed me by the shoulders and steered me around to the driver's side, holding the door open while I lowered myself into the seat. 'We talked about it, Doll. It's going to be good. It's a good idea.' He shut the door and smiled at me through the window. I buckled myself in, started the car and wondered exactly how many seconds it'd take him to boot up the Xbox after I drove away.

'It's a good idea,' I repeated Kyle's words to myself. I was the one who'd encouraged him to use the time alone to relax, do something that he enjoyed. I wasn't into video games myself, had always lacked the necessary hand-eye coordination, but I understood the appeal. A dopamine-spiked world of lights and sounds and endless opportunities to start again.

* * *

Kyle says I could sleep through a hurricane. Any hope this would change once the baby arrived, that some sort of maternal instinct would kick in, was squashed by my second night at the Royal Women's.

'Time to feed the baby.' The young midwife shook me awake; her tone was firm. 'You've been asleep for five hours.'

I preferred the older midwives. They called you 'sweetheart' and 'darl'. The 20-something graduates were fun, but unsympathetic. The way they plunged their fingers into my abdomen each day took my breath away. I could've been anything, dead or alive – they could've been digging in a garden bed.

At home, though, I had Kyle. If the baby so much as farted, Kyle woke immediately. He would change the baby's nappy and bring him to me in bed, and all I had to do was plug the baby's mouth with my nipple. And stay awake. That was the difficult part. On balance, Kyle got far less sleep, but he was still working, cleaning, holding trains of thought and threads of conversation. I was barely functioning.

It was my mother who had suggested that the baby and I go and stay with her for the long weekend. A 'sleep holiday', she called it. For three days she would do everything, she said. For three days Kyle and I could get some sleep. Kyle immediately agreed.

'For both our sakes, Doll. For the baby.'

* * *

I'd been going for my daily walks since the day I got home, as instructed by the in-hospital physio. I applied myself to those gruelling two-hundred-metre treks like I was studying for an exam I desperately needed to pass. The first one I alternated between sobbing and laughing at how unhinged I must've looked, hobbling around the neighbourhood in my pyjama pants.

After a couple of weeks, I worked up the mental and physical strength to venture out with the pram for the first time. I arranged to meet a friend at Carlton Gardens. The pram was awkward and bulky. It wasn't an extension of my body yet, like my huge belly had been. How had I ever learned to live with a giant watermelon jammed under my shirt? How was I now, suddenly, supposed to live without it?

I wasn't far from home when I came to a stop at the kerb to let a few cars pass before crossing. But I didn't judge it right. I can still see the woman's face in the window as her car sailed past me. So close. Too close. I knew my expression would have mirrored hers as we both realised my mistake; we both thought she was going to hit the pram.

Somehow, I made it to the park to meet my friend. We kissed hello and peered into the blanketed caves of each other's prams before rolling out our picnic blankets and placing our babies in between us on their backs, two upended turtles. I have no idea what we talked about, but my friend didn't seem to notice that I wasn't really there. I arranged my face in the appropriate expressions, and responded to her using the required words in the correct order, and I tried to ignore the image of the car and the woman's face each time it flashed into my mind. At the first sign of fussiness from the baby I scooped him up from the ground and made an excuse to leave. I texted Kyle that I was on my way home and when I arrived he was standing on the front step, waiting for me. I made it all the way to the gate before I lost it, rushing up the front steps and pushing past Kyle into the hallway. He collected the pram from the footpath and brought it, and the baby, inside.

I shut myself in the bedroom and lay down on the bed. I squeezed my eyelids closed but the woman's face in the car window was still there, staring back at me. I pressed down on my eyelids with my fingers. The image replayed and replayed, until the woman's face became my face, and it was me in the car, speeding away from that other dishevelled, terrible woman at the side of the road. I took out my phone and scrolled and scrolled, looking for other images that might erase the car and the window and the face. After 30 minutes of that, the baby let out a sharp cry from wherever he was in the house. My legs carried me from the bedroom and into the kitchen. My arms tugged the baby from Kyle's arms. My body moved on its own, summoned by the baby's cries.

I took the baby to the couch, positioned him on the breastfeeding pillow and within seconds he clamped on tight and sucked, his eyes staring straight ahead, supremely focused. I wasn't ready to stop beating myself up yet. I had known him for less than two months, how could I be sure this was really my baby, alive and well and lying in my arms? What were his distinguishing features? That he was tiny? That he was mine? Looking at him it was clear he was both of those things. A familiar tide of possession swelled up in me, but I couldn't shake the feeling that he *shouldn't* be here, because of what I did. And yet like Crash Bandicoot after falling down a dark hole, like Mario after sailing off the side of a candy-coloured cliff in his Kart, my baby had reappeared.

My breast felt soft and empty, so I broke the tight seal of his lips with my little finger and rolled him off to the side. He lay across my legs, looking up at me, stupefied and full.

'How many lives do you have left?' I asked him.

Baby number two returned a small drunken smile.

* * *

Kyle had started seeing an ecopsychologist around the time he sold his car. When he told me, saying it was for his anger problem, I laughed. (Kyle was the sort of person unimaginative people described as a gentle giant.) I stopped laughing pretty quick once I realised it wasn't a joke. He said he was angry at everyone, all the time. It was interfering with work, with everything.

'It's like people think there are chances after this. But there aren't,' he said. 'Everyone's living in a fantasy land.'

Perhaps if he did what normal repressed people do and take it out on those closest to him I would've known this was going on. But it just went on inside of him, in private. He'd been able to keep it under control so far, he said. He told me he felt like a bomb.

* * *

The sleep holiday was a month after the pram incident. By that point I'd stopped tiptoeing around the baby, waiting for the other shoe to drop. I forgot to regard him with suspicion. I was too relaxed, which is probably what allowed me to get behind the wheel and drive to my mother's house in the first place. It's only a 15-minute drive, Kyle encouraged me. He suggested I put on a podcast, one of those grim true crime ones I liked, to help keep me focussed.

The sun was warm through the window that morning. I'd had some solid hours the night before, and a sleep-in after the morning feed. I shouldn't have been particularly tired. Except that one moment I was driving along, and the next I opened my eyes, still driving, and there were seconds I couldn't account for.

I pulled over at the first opportunity, into a petrol station on St George's Road, and called my mother. I told her where I was and that she had to come and collect me.

'Don't tell Kyle,' I said when she got into the driver's seat beside me. I had already moved across to the passenger side. Once mum was driving, I mustered up the courage to look behind me into the special mirror we'd fitted to the headrest so we could see the baby's face. He stared at me with his round eyes, sucking intently on his dummy. Baby number three.

I called Kyle the next morning. He told me he'd had the best sleep of his life.

'You were right, this was a great idea,' I said. 'I feel better already.'

That was a couple of weeks ago, now. This morning we were walking with the pram, drinking takeaway coffee from our reusable cups. Kyle had white spots of froth stuck to individual hairs of his moustache. Was he angry now? He was always angry, I remembered. But it was Sunday morning, he was drinking a $6 oat milk flat white, the sun was shining.

'What's he going to be like, do you think?' I asked. Kyle held his coffee in one hand and pushed the pram with the other. I trotted a bit to keep up. 'Like, will he grow up to be a contestant on a cooking show? Or a dentist? Maybe he'll take after you, play footy.'

'I hope not.' Kyle took another sip of his coffee and manoeuvred the pram around a too-slow couple and their whippet. I fell behind, caught up again.

'Well, what do *you* reckon then?'

He sighed. 'I dunno, Doll. What do you want me to say?'

'Geez. It wasn't meant to be a test.'

'Well, it feels a bit like one. I don't think like you do, imagining fake scenarios.'

I had annoyed him. Disappointed him with my trivial concerns. Another idiot talking about a future that didn't exist. I looked down at the baby, baby number three, and that feeling rose up in me again, possession, anchoring me to this person, to this earth. Also, relief. Because my clever baby had figured it out. Kyle just couldn't see it, not yet.

I looked around at the other people on the street, the people that made my husband so angry. I watched them as they went about their lives, throwing their single-use coffee cups in the bin, driving their two cars around. I considered telling Kyle that maybe they knew something he didn't. Maybe there were more chances. Maybe I knew it too.

Spring

Kim Waters

Spring sneaks up on us before its due date.
The jonquils push their crayon crowns
up through the earth. The grass grows
hungry for attention. The clouds explode,
their milky stains powdering a pale blue sky.

Spring stages a sit-in, throws down the gauntlet,
dares anyone to stop it in its tracks. The air
sneezes as the colours come out to play.
It has the tulip line down pat and there's
nectar cradled in the fontanelles of buds.

My Summer as a Vampire

Lev Verlaine

With legs boiled over bedside
I know why
     that
sometimes I wish I'd just wake a dying man
     and have an ending certainty that I can see.

The mirror,   (there's no mirror)
     says
bruiser boy, step forward
show us the knuckles that spread like God and put to sleep.

     Summer feels like suicide. Must be
why everything I touch gets some heat about it.

Her moon beams down at me from eve blue sky
     says
I don't wear my skin well enough and I don't recognise it.

     He's spit of his father and he has to live with it
   forever.
       At least he belonged to a good
    mother.

My eyes are getting worse the longer I stay in the dark.

            Is the end of June the right time to meet
    someone?

            Is it too much to ask for somewhere to
    come home to?

I try to look for people in others,

        everyone is known.

I'm looking for someone who

        can remind me of myself

but there is no one and I am alone.

29

Some Day

Natalie Cooper

The blood, sweat and tears of rebellious women
smear the history of mankind. As these
valorous women have spent their precious lives
resisting, derailing and fighting the suffocating layers
of oppression. Distorted and bigoted restrictions forced
upon women, in an attempt to confine us to nothing more
than a life of servitude.

To these divinely defiant women, these honourable
headstrong heroines, I am eternally grateful for their grit,
spunk and beautiful noncompliance in the face of life as a
second-class citizen. Smacking the antiquated mandates
from the choking grasp of our oppressors' predacious hands.

I ponder though, as the seasons of life ebb and flow,
what will the history books delineate about me and my life?
Will I be remembered as an insipid so and so, who was too
timid to advocate? Or a sadly surrendered, broken-down
woman, feeble and muted?

Hell no!

I want to be recounted as an unshakable nonconformist,
who never ceased to extricate women's autonomy from the
grimy clutches of moth-eaten, monochrome men.
Forever striving to cast in stone equality for female folk
of all persuasions.

I want my legacy to echo that of history's most fantastically
insubordinate women. The likes of–
Malala and her shatterproof strength,
The powerful persistence of Greta,
Frida's courageous creativity and
The insightful intelligence of Ada.
I want this freethinking tenacity to course through the veins
of my descendants. Priming them to continue fighting, until–
Some day,
Hopefully sooner than later, they don't need to be chronically
vigilant anymore. Instead, they can enjoy a happy peaceful
existence without mummifying restrictions shrivelling their
lives. As equity will have materialised and at long last–
Women will be liberated.

30

Bollards

Kim Waters

The streets are lined with stainless steel bollards,
shrines to those with unholy intent. Searching
for populated settings, they jack-knife their way

into arenas where people gather and what binds
a community together is easily undone
by a disaffected person in a stolen van for whom

the wick of incendiary marks their territory.
And with a conscience pulled free of its grip,
another dark monument is engraved in history.

Once their thimble-shaped domes appeared
as jaunty lifeguards, kiss-curl bob bathing beauties
and barbershop men with handlebar mustaches.

Now, on every corner a security camera waits
to record the grainy actions of a deviant, who
his neighbours will say seemed *perfectly normal.*

Signposts warn of abandoned bags left on busy streets,
train stations and the corridors of airports. A day
in the city and we come armed with safety mobile apps

and a fist of bundled keys. When tragedy occurs
we lay kerbstone wreaths to douse the scent of blood.
Undeterred, the mourners join hands, wanting

to believe in the strength of a human daisy chain.

31

Wool

M.A. Quigley

There's a mistake in the front of the jumper I'm knitting for my husband, John. I unravel the wool. Our cat, Tabitha, wakes from her nap and thinks I'm playing a game. She prances across the carpet in the living room, and her paws pounce on the ball of wool. There's something about her hyperactive behaviour and the fun she's having that takes me back in time to when I was young.

Mum sat in the living room knitting a jumper for Dad, and my sister and I wanted to learn. She taught us how to make a scarf of our football colours. I've still got the black and yellow scarf in my bottom drawer in the cupboard. I've worn it to every match with a sense of pride.

Back then, I couldn't name the feelings that stirred within me, like when my grandmother grabbed either side of my face and pinched my cheeks with her thumb and forefinger before kissing me. My future was unfathomable, playing out day by day. Now, I hold onto each day, trying to control the unforeseeable and uncontrollable.

I unwind some more wool, and Tabitha's paws flick at it gleefully. She's unaware of what's happening apart from the connection to control. Any other time, I'd laugh and think she was funny, but my patience is dissipating. It's then that I realise that she'll become part of our treasured memories, and I wonder whether we'll fight to see who gets to keep her.

John started going out on a Saturday afternoon a few months ago to help a friend renovate his house. At first, I didn't think anything of it until the same friend rang and wanted to speak to him.

'He's at work. Give him a call on his mobile,' I said, wondering what the hell he was doing.

I now know where John goes because I've followed him. He leaves home at the same time. He's been seeing another woman, and she has a child. John was holding the woman's hand. Her child held a fluffy toy and tottered close. I felt like a steamroller had ridden over my chest. I wanted to run toward them and yell at him, why are you doing this to me? To us? Something made me hold back. How could I've been such a fool not to read him better?

What does he see in her? She looks like a younger version of me with the same build and colour hair. Is it because I'm older now and he doesn't find me attractive anymore? They were in full view of me, but I don't think they knew that I was watching them because there were so many people around us in the park. I picked up my mobile to ring a friend to ask her if she'd seen him. I know that she takes her children to the park. I placed my phone back on the table. If she hasn't seen him, then she'll know. Either way, I'm the one who loses. Each time he comes home, I ask him how his friend's renovations are coming along, and he has the same reply: good.

I ponder where we went wrong. In the beginning, we used to see one another every night. When we married, I thought I'd found someone to be with me for the rest of my life. Sex was good, and over time he'd complain that he was tired. Now, there is no chemistry between us. He no longer wants to hug or talk to me. All I need to hear are three words he used to say to me all the time: I love you. I can't understand why he has become as untouchable as the moon. I haven't been single for ten years, and whenever I say let's do something together, he makes excuses.

We used to sit up until all hours sipping wine and talking. We were drunk on our mutual love of art and literature, the galleries we wanted to visit, and the books we hadn't read yet. I tell myself I still feel the same way about John, but something is different. It was like we were sitting in a void. Now, I ask myself: who is this man that I once knew? The fluidity of our relationship has receded as well as our aspirations. Now we are like strangers who show mutual respect whenever we are in each other's company.

Tabitha pulls harder. Time stops and reminds me of when I played tug of war with a piece of rope with my sister and our friends. We were having fun, laughing, and squealing with excitement as we tried to pull one another over the line. I unravel some more wool. Tabitha moves it back and forth playfully. Those days are precious memories which is what John will soon become.

I've lost control over the ball of wool. Tabitha ducks and weaves, like John tends to do if I ask him any questions. I long to know what this man I married thinks. My mind wanders back to my 7th birthday when my sister and our friends played pin the tail on the donkey. Mum put the blindfold on me, and I had the dart in my hand, ready to make my mark. Earlier, I'd watched her and Dad holding hands and kissing. I wanted to be married in a loving relationship when I grew up and have children like them. I believed I had made my mark and could have what my parents had when I met John. We could grow old together and still be in love, but now I don't know what to think.

When I was single, I didn't understand that trying to have children could rip a marriage apart. When John and I were dating, we had many friends. Now we have few. Dad said as we got older, good friends would be hard to find. All our friends were lucky enough to have children.

In the beginning, they asked us if we were going to have any children. Our reply was always the same: we will. One friend said we wouldn't understand what they were going through because we didn't have any. Whenever we suggested going out, they were too busy. They no longer asked us any questions. Our only focus was IVF.

I fell pregnant and miscarried at twelve weeks. On my next attempt, I had a phantom pregnancy. More eggs were retrieved, and I had two of them inserted. My hormones were a graph going up and down that I had no control over. The placenta was growing inside of me, but no baby. The specialist said that we were too old to have children. We refused to believe him and kept trying on our own because we were too old to adopt. We thought we were managing our new life without children. Now, apart from Tabitha, my world is empty.

I run after Tabitha. She's underneath the kitchen table. The wool is a tangled mess, and I try to get the ball from her, but it's a struggle. I'm tied in a moment of reflection before she swipes my hand with her paws and moves away. I tell myself that I'll be able to cope. I can hear a noise outside and walk into the living room and open the blinds wider. A woman is walking past our house with a pram. Two young boys are talking and laughing beside her. They all seem happy, and I know I'm telling lies. I won't be able to manage without John. I long for him to wrap his arms around me and tell me everything will be okay. My mind is full of doubt and uncertainty about our future and what it will bring. It scares me.

In our bedroom, I lie on my stomach, trying to coax Tabitha out from under the bed, but she won't budge. The wool is no longer a jumper or ball. Tabitha's claws have ripped it into several pieces. I stand up and peer out the window. The sky has turned grey. In the kitchen, I open a can of cat food. The weather of our marriage has changed, and the divide is getting wider. I fill Tabitha's bowl with food, and she comes into the kitchen purring around my legs. I place the bowl on the floor before retrieving the wool, wondering if tonight will be the night when he says goodbye.

Contributors

Editors

Samuel Bernard is a freelance writer, critic and editor. He writes for *The Weekend Australian* as a literary critic, and is a monthly contributor to their 'Notable Books' column. Samuel also writes features, criticism and a monthly column for *Good Reading Magazine*. He has a Master of Writing and is completing a PhD in Creative Writing at Monash University.

Thomas Rock is completing a PhD in Creative Writing at Monash University. His thesis examines optimism in contemporary Australian young-adult science fiction. He works in a primary-school library in regional Victoria.

Vera Yingzhi Gu has a PhD in Translation Studies and is an interpreting instructor in the Master of Interpreting and Translation Studies at Monash University. Vera has a strong research interest in translation and interpreting pedagogy. She is a professional-level translator and interpreter in Chinese/Mandarin and English language pairs and a conference interpreter by training.

Authors

Carmel Bird grew up in Tasmania, and much of her writing reflects the influence of her origins. Her earliest stories were published in *The Women's Weekly* in the 1960s. She has written eight collections of stories, with the latest, *Love Letter to Lola*, to be published in 2023. Her most recent novel is *Field of Poppies* (2019), and her memoir, *Telltale*, was published in 2022. http://www.carmelbird.com/

Ahimsa Timoteo Bodhrán is the author of *Archipiélagos*; *Antes y después del Bronx: Lenapehoking*; and *South Bronx Breathing Lessons*; editor of the international queer Indigenous issue of *Yellow Medicine Review: A Journal* *of Indigenous Literature, Art, and Thought*; and co-editor of the Native dance/ movement/performance issue of *Movement Research Performance Journal*. His work appears in Australia in *Antithesis, dotdotdash, Etchings, Going Down Swinging, Griffith Review, Idiom 23, Island, Kurungabaa, Otoliths, Rabbit, Regime, Sketch, Verandah* and *Windmills*; and Aotearoa in *Bravado, brief, Catalyst, Enamel, Landfall* and *Poetry New Zealand*.

Sofia Chapman completed a Languages BA (Hons) in Tasmania before running away to play accordion on a French theatre barge. Returning to Australia Sofia studied playwriting and joined the band Vardos. Sofia's queer plays include the award-winning *The Four Accordionists of the Apocalypse*. Sofia's stories, cartoons, short films and radio plays appear internationally and she is shortlisted for the 2022 Dorothy Porter Poetry Prize.

Lucy Connelly is a Year 12 student in Gippsland. She has enjoyed her study of Literature, Philosophy and Studio Art throughout VCE, and is looking forward to continuing this study in university. Her art and poetry is largely inspired by thinkers such as Anne Sexton, Sylvia Plath, Vincent van Gogh and Friedrich Nietzsche.

Natalie Cooper is an early childhood educator and picture book enthusiast who spends her days wrangling children and her nights writing poetry. Currently Natalie resides on Woiwurrung Country with her trio of mischief-making children and partner in crime husband.

Koraly Dimitriadis is a writer, performer and the author of the poetry books *Just Give Me The Pills* and *Love and F--k Poems*, an Australian poetry bestseller which has also been translated to Greek. Her literary writing has been published in Czech, Polish and Greek journals, and locally in journals such as *Meanjin* and *Southerly*. Koraly makes films and theatre with her poems. Her opinion articles have been published widely, including in *The Washington Post, The Guardian, Al Jazeera* and *The Independent*. She received the UNESCO Literature residency (Krakow) for her fiction manuscript, 'We Never Said Goodbye'. She is researching a book of non-fiction, 'Not Till You're Married', supported by Creative Victoria.

Elena Disilvestro is a Venezuelan-Australian writer making her publishing debut with 'Chimaera', a story of female defiance. Venturing into the world of fantasy horror, she aims to provide a narrative as gruesome as it is compelling.

Jane Downing's stories and poems have been published around Australia and overseas, including in *Griffith Review*, *Big Issue*, *Antipodes*, *Southerly*, *Westerly*, *Island*, *Overland*, *Meanjin*, *Canberra Times*, *Cordite*, *Best Australian Poems*, and previously in *Verge*. She has a Doctor of Creative Arts degree from the University of Technology, Sydney, the creative component of which, *The Sultan's Daughter*, was released by Obiter Publishing in 2020.

Merav Fima is currently completing her PhD in Creative Writing at Monash University. Her prose and poetry have appeared in a number of anthologies and literary journals, including *Verge*, *Colloquy* and *Meanjin Quarterly*. Her short story 'Bride Immaculate' won the first prize in the Energheia Literary Competition in Matera, Italy (2014), and 'Rose among the Thorns' was a finalist in the *Tiferet* literary journal's 2019 fiction contest. She is the translator of Gal Ventura's scholarly monograph, *Maternal Breast-Feeding and Its Substitutes in Nineteenth-Century French Art* (Brill, 2018). She has recently completed a collection of short stories and is now at work on her first novel and a memoir.

Jenny Hedley's narrative nonfiction was shortlisted for the 2022 Lord Mayor's Creative Writing Awards. Her writing appears in *Admissions: Voices within Mental Health*, *Overland*, *Cordite Poetry Review*, *DIAGRAM*, *Mascara Literary Review*, *Verity La*, *Archer* and *Westerly*. She lives on unceded Boon Wurrung land with her son. Website: jennyhedley.github.io/

Melanie Hutchinson is an emerging writer who recently completed her Master of Literature and Creative Writing degree at Deakin University. When not writing, she is a violinist masquerading as a technology lawyer. Born and raised in Australia, she has enjoyed several years living in Asia, Europe and travelling the globe but is now settled in Ngunnawal Country with family and two fur babies.

Angela Jones is a writer, musician, artist and academic from Perth, Western Australia. She is currently enrolled as a PhD student in creative writing at Monash University, Melbourne, Australia. Angela is a published author in the fields of popular cultural studies and education, but her true joy is writing poetry, campus fiction and magic realist fiction. She loves to weave taboo subjects into a tale of whim, or play a literary riff through the rhyme and rhythm of 60s-inspired Beat poetry.

Deborah Lee adores poetry and stories. She calls her middle sister B and has been drawn to B-towns such as Ballarat, Brunswick and Brisbane, Australia. Publications include *Cicerone Journal*, *Consilience*, *fourW*, *Grieve* anthology, *Page Seventeen*, *Paradise Anthology*, *Pink Panther Magazine*, *Pressure Gauge* journal, *The Sciku Project*, *Stereo Stories*.

Tessa Martin is 19 years of age and studying a Bachelor of Education (Honours) and a Bachelor of Arts, majoring in Literary Studies. She currently works in a school and hopes to become a Secondary English and Drama teacher. Her love of theatre and poetry has heavily influenced her writing development. She has had a passion for words since she was young and is particularly interested in romanticising everyday life through writing and addressing large sociological topics. Her writing takes the form of narrative, poetry and theatre, and she hopes to publish her own novel and poetry collection one day. Instagram: poetry_of_may.

Lilly O'Gorman is a writer and communications officer. She studied Journalism and English at Monash University and is a graduate of the Faber Writing Academy. She lives in Melbourne on Wurundjeri land with her husband and son.

M.A. Quigley lives in Melbourne, Victoria with her husband and two dogs. She completed an Associate Degree in Professional Writing and Editing at RMIT University in Melbourne, Australia in 2015. Her flash fiction, poetry and short stories have been published in twenty-five anthologies, in the Philippines, the US, Canada, the UK, India and Australia. Her debut novel, *The Complexities of Love*, was published by a traditional publisher in Canada in August 2021. When she's not writing she loves doing yoga and cooking.

Isabelle Quilty (she/they) is a nonbinary writer and poet from regional NSW, Australia. Some of their work is published under Beau Quilty. Most of their work is based around LGBTQ+ topics, working towards a greener future and works inspired by their South Asian ancestry. They've been published in a variety of magazines including *Spineless Wonders*, *Kindling and Sage*, *Mascara Literary Review* and *Demure Magazine*. Their work has been adapted into a concert titled 'Carved by Mountains'. They also have a bachelor's degree in Writing and Publishing.

Charlotte Romeo is a fantasy, contemporary fiction and romance author located in Victoria, Australia. She debuted in the writing industry with her short story 'Phoenix Rising'. When Charlotte isn't impulsively beginning yet another writing project, she is a lover of health and wellbeing, podcasts, learning languages and eating delicious food. Charlotte can be found on Instagram @charlotte_romeo_

Ashleigh K. Rose is a WA-born and -raised poet, with a Bachelor of Arts in Mass Communications and a Graduate Certificate in Human Rights. Purpose-driven by adding value to the lives of others, by day she does this working in the community development space – by night, through poetry. Her poetry has been published in a range of online and print anthologies, journals and publications.

Paris Rosemont is a performance poet whose poetry features in publications including *FemAsia Magazine*, Red Room Poetry's *Admissions* anthology and *Heroines Anthology* (vol.4). Paris was longlisted for the Joyce Parkes Prize 2022 and was the winner of the Poetry Prize for the New England Thunderbolt Prize for Crime Writing 2022. She has performed her original poetry at various events, including the Sydney Fringe Festival 2022. Paris has been a Living Stories Competition judge, a WestWords Academian and writer-in-residence, as well as a Frontier Poetry scholarship recipient. She was awarded an Arts Access Australia mentorship, a WestWords/Varuna Emerging Writers' Residency and was named runner up for the Writing NSW x Varuna Fellowship 2022. Paris is thrilled to have been awarded a Westwords/Copyright Agency Fellowship 2023 and hopes to publish her debut poetry collection in the not-too-distant-future.

Cameron Semmens is a connoisseur of fine words, a poet and author, a soul plumber, a force of dadness to three kids, and a hope-oriented wonder-monger living in Melbourne. He's a passionate poetry educator, running workshops for students and adults across Australia. He has published 27 books – his latest release is *10 Poems I Like …Maybe You'll Like 'Em Too!* – and he's released five spoken word albums, has had many individual poems published in magazines and journals, and currently hosts two podcasts: *Shards* and *The Persian and The Poet*. Check out www.webcameron.com for more details and info.

Ibtisam Shahbaz is an emerging writer and poet based in Naarm. Her work is influenced by the amalgamation of her childhood in Australia and Pakistani heritage. She has a passion for literature and prose and is currently working on her manuscript for a poetry collection. She has volunteered with Red Room Poetry, working on their annual Poetry Month and Poem Forest projects. You can find more about her writing journey at www.ibtisamshahbaz.com or on @ibtisampoetry.

Warwick Sprawson is a Melbourne-based writer. His work has appeared in many publications including *Meanjin*, *Southerly*, *Westerly*, *Page 17* and *The Fiction Desk*. A keen hiker, he has published guidebooks to Tasmania's Overland Track and Victoria's Great South West Walk.

Kellie Tori is an actor, theatre director and emerging writer based in Melbourne/Naarm. She is passionate about developing new writing in her theatre practice and has extensive experience directing spoken word / storytelling shows. She has always written poetry but is very new to sharing it.

Arwen Verdnik (she/her) is an emerging writer from Naarm/Melbourne. Her creative work explores the intricacies of memory and the fragility of child-hood innocence. She has volunteered as an intern at *Australian Book Review* and her poetry has been published in *Lot's Wife*. She is commencing Literary Studies (Honours) at Monash University in 2023 and plays volleyball in her spare time.

Lev Verlaine is a trans poet based in Washington state. He balances his inspiration between experiences in transgenderism and his love of nature and the human world. His works have appeared in Querencia Press.

Kim Waters lives in Melbourne. She has a Master of Arts in creative writing. She uses art, music and walks with her dog as inspiration for her poems. Some of those poems have appeared in *The Australian*, *Going Down Swinging Online*, *Not Very Quiet* and *The Shanghai Literary Review*.

.

CPSIA information can be obtained
at www.ICGtesting.com
Printed in the USA
BVHW032009160223
658709BV00002B/36